GW00724770

2

PENGUIN BOOKS
CLASSICAL MUSIC

Joy Cowley lives with her husband Terry in the
Marlborough Sounds along with eight cats and seventy
sheep.

This is her first adult novel for many years although
she is one of New Zealand's most loved children's
writers and a frequent award winner. She is also famous
here and all over North America for her hundreds of
wonderful children's readers.

ACKNOWLEDGEMENTS

Writing, paradoxically, is a form of communication which takes place in solitude. As such it can be a lonely occupation. I owe more gratitude than I can express to the English faculty of Massey University, New Zealand, who have given me warm encouragement and support for many years.

Gratitude also to Tom and Linda Krueger of The Maple Inn, Chautauqua, NY, who gave me place and space in which to write this book, and to dear Terry who read the whole thing over my shoulder, as it emerged.

CLASSICAL MUSIC

Joy Cowley

PENGUIN BOOKS

PENGUIN BOOKS

Penguin Books (NZ) Ltd, cnr Airborne and Rosedale Roads, Albany,
Auckland 1310, New Zealand
Penguin Books Ltd, 27 Wrights Lane, London W8 5TZ, England
Penguin USA, 375 Hudson Street, New York, NY 10014, United States
Penguin Books Australia Ltd, 487 Maroondah Highway, Ringwood, Australia 3134
Penguin Books Canada Ltd, 10 Alcorn Avenue, Toronto, Ontario, Canada M4V 3B2
Penguin Books (South Africa) Pty Ltd, 4 Pallinghurst Road, Parktown,
Johannesburg 2193, South Africa
Penguin Books India (P) Ltd, 11, Community Centre, Panchsheel Park,
New Delhi 110 017, India

Penguin Books Ltd, Registered Offices: Harmondsworth, Middlesex, England

First published by Penguin Books (NZ) Ltd, 1999

3 5 7 9 10 8 6 4

Designed and typeset by Mary Egan, Egan-Reid Ltd
Printed in Australia by Australian Print Group, Maryborough

Front cover photograph Alexander Turnbull Library, National Library of
New Zealand, Te Puna Mātauranga o Aotearoa. Two girls eating ice creams,
30 Sept, 1944. Photographer, John Dobree Pascoe, 1908–1972. Ref: F–1269–1/4.
Image colourised from a black and white photograph.

*For Anne McCormick who edited my first novel,
in celebration of 34 years of friendship.*

1
DELIA

My father is dead and it is raining.

There was rain at my mother's graveside service, a great symphony of a storm played from dark cloud. I remember the air full of violin bows, timpani and woodwinds, and I was held by the thought that all music came from a hollowness. The emptiness of the instrument was essentially its voice and its beauty. I wanted to apply that to life as some kind of philosophical balm for grief but it didn't work. The words too, were as empty as the vast New Zealand sky, which poured itself out on our black umbrellas and drummed without respect against the lid of the casket.

But today there is a small Manhattan sky, comfortable, contained by towers, a patchwork quilt of even grey. You don't feel threatened by a sky packaged like this. At no time do you get the feeling that the entire universe is about to suck you up like a vacuum-cleaner. The towers hem you about with the reassurance of a well-structured fort and even forty-three floors up, all you see of infinity is a few squares of security blanket softened by mist. It has been raining all day, gentle but persistent. There is more mist below, shredded across the East river, which is as dark as old aluminium.

The desk phone is humming, my sister Beatrice calling from New Zealand.

I still say *aluMINium*. I still say *aDRESS* and *windscreen* and occasionally, in self-defence, *petrol*. The old New Zealand English is hoarded like a collection of childhood toys in the attic and although they are not particularly attractive toys, I will not be rid of them. In the honesty of middle age I claim a fondness for some security blankets, along with the right to discard others.

Hum-hum, hum-hum. The answering-machine is not turned on, no tinkle of J S Bach and a welcome to the home of Delia Munro and Associates, Interiors. The phone is white, faintly opalescent and its call is pitched at the mother tone of the human voice. That was Lal's idea. He says that sound should massage the soul. If he had his way, all the phones in the office would be chanting Om.

I stand at the window and wonder how they will manage without me. There are several big jobs coming up, including the complete makeover of the 34th Street brownstone, the redecoration of Sporting Life 2000, the Poughkeepsie apart-ments, and I will definitely have to go, probably tomorrow morning.

Forty-two floors beneath my feet, bugs crawl through wet canyons, escaping from the afternoon, yellow taxis, limos, a weaving ambulance frantic with lights. Hum-hum. Okay, Bea. Hum-hum. Okay.

'Diddy? Is that you?' Her voice is close and very small.

'Hello Bea.'

'Diddy, it's Dad. He's gone.'

I already know, Bea. I knew forty, no, forty-three minutes ago. Should I tell you? I'd gotten half way through Waddison Fabrics' new price list, when the office was full of him, his energy, his sweat, tobacco breath, the sour mud of his socks.

Not the old man in the nursing home, Bea, but him, out of the rain from feeding hay to the sheep and holding us one in each arm against his tartan jacket, his face and hair dripping on us. I could actually feel him, Bea. I could breathe him in.

'Diddy, are you there?'

'Sure, Bea. When did it happen?'

'This morning. Not long, about a quarter past eight, we think. I wasn't there, Diddy, I'd been with him all night and I'd just gone out for a cup of coffee. The doctor said that sometimes happens. They slip away when the family. Diddy, they lost his teeth. How could they do that? He hasn't got any and his face. Well, there's no point in getting new dentures now is there? When are you coming home?'

'As soon as I can get a flight. Tomorrow, probably. Have you spoken with the priest and the funeral director?'

'When would I have talked to the funeral director?' Her voice gets thinner. 'I'm on my own here, Diddy. Father O'Donnell's gone and the doctor. I mean they're all so busy. Frank's in Sydney. He hates me calling him Frank. He hasn't been home since last Christmas and I believe she's expecting again. She doesn't call me Mum, you know. I wouldn't ask her to but it's the way she says Beatrice as though it's got a rotten taste. Well, that's the way it is and you're in New York. Aunty Em's just had a pin put in her hip and anyway she's. They didn't call it Alzheimer's when we were young. It was second childhood. The Rawiris have been a tower of strength but really there's a limit. Diddy, it's been so long, five and a half years.'

'I know. I know, Bea.'

'No, you don't. The last time you saw him at least he could recognise you. You don't know. You're worse than Frank. A postcard when you feel like it. When you think you've got time but find out you haven't.' Her words are scratched with tears. 'They don't know where they put his teeth. You know what I reckon? Someone else is wearing them. Rammed in some poor old soul's mouth.'

While she talks about the nursing home, I shuffle words, trying to select something that will fit my experience, the visitation if you like to call it that. I want to tell her but I must be careful, otherwise she'll blow it up like a Macy's parade balloon and paint religion all over it. Maybe it wasn't my father's spirit in the office, but a trick of memory. Maybe the moment of death broke some genetic linkage which sent a ripple through me, a small fracture in time the moment the clock stopped ticking, and my imagination picked up on it. I knew my father was dead. That is certain. But I don't know with the same certainty that his spirit was in my office. I lean into the phone and her weeping, picking up the role of older sister. 'I'm on my way, Bea. Promise. I'll book a flight as soon as I hang up and then it's only forty-eight hours.'

'How long will you stay? Three weeks?'

'We no, no, I'm afraid –'

'You always say next time it'll be three weeks. Why do you keep saying that? In twenty-six years it hasn't been three weeks, hasn't –'

'Bea, I think I can manage to get away for a week. When's the funeral?'

'Father O'Donnell's suggested Saturday but that's got to fit in with the undertaker. I'm seeing him at ten o'clock. I've got to make all the decisions, Diddy, so I just hope you don't think. When can you get here?'

'Friday morning, if I get on the flight. You'll do fine, Bea. Before you know it, we'll be talking over a bottle of wine instead of the phone. Do you still drink cabernet merlot?'

She sniffs. 'It gives me a headache. What time is it over there? I forget.'

'Ten after four, Tuesday.'

'It's Wednesday morning here. Tuesday he was still breathing. Funny, his hands were cold but not his face. His cheeks were rosy pink like a baby's and his breath was warm, sort of slow and empty. What flight did you say?'

'I'll call you back as soon as I know. Where are you staying? I suggest you go to bed. I can leave a message on your answering machine.'

'I can't, Diddy. There's too much to do.'

'You won't be able to organise anything in a state of exhaustion. Let it wait. Take a tablet. Switch on the electric blanket.'

'Diddy, it's midsummer!' She laughs wetly. 'You forgot that, didn't you? I'll bet it's cold over there right now. Snow a metre deep.'

'Well, no, just a chill misty rain. Look, Bea, I've got to finish this call and do some planning.'

'I'm sorry, Diddy. I didn't mean to go on at you. It's just that. Well, you were here when Mum died. There were the three of us. You and me and him. This time. But the Rawiris have been simply marvellous. Did I tell you? And Molly Gleave who does the flowers. The staff of course. But it's not the same as a partner, Diddy. It's funny but I miss Barry. He was the one so good at legal and technical thingies.'

'What about Ralston?'

'Who?'

'Ralston? Rawson? Your chef?'

Silence. Sometimes she holds her breath to think. Then comes the sigh full in my ear. 'You're so lucky, Diddy. You've got Lal to do things for you.'

Lal a doer? I smile and cup my hands around the phone. 'Bea, I have to call the airlines. There are a million things to organise.'

'You will pray for his soul?'

11

I lift the Waddison fabric list and put it down again. 'Hey, you know –'

'Diddy, it's what I believe. It's what he believed.'

'Sure, Bea. Will you give me your number?'

When the call is over, I move back to the windows and realise that the city has turned its lights on. The shawls of mist are dyed orange, pink and green, and streams of traffic, as dense as Christmas tree garlands, barely ripple the colours in the big puddle that covers the intersection of 48th and Lexington. The sidewalks and crosswalks blossom umbrellas.

It's not so much a prayer as an apology for the lack of it, the absence of any kind of feeling, religious or otherwise. I tell the city, 'You're okay, Dad. Everyone dies. That's life. Trust it.'

In the outer office my new secretary Momo is leaning over some blueprints on her desk. Her hair falls over her face like a black silk curtain. Her skin, unmarked by expression, has the fragile glow of porcelain. In that whiteness, her eyes seem very dark, her mouth redder than blood. In the six weeks she has been here, she has caused seismic vibrations amongst some of the staff.

'Momo, please, some airline reservations for myself, United first flight tomorrow morning to LA and then Air New Zealand tomorrow night to Auckland. From Auckland it's the first flight to Napier.'

She opens her phone pad with a jab of a long black nail and says, 'Round ticket?'

'Yes. Of course. To return on the tenth, six days from now.' I have been tempted to suggest that she exchange her attorney boyfriend for a poet with a briefcase full of fresh metaphor. But I suspect that she despises sentiment, even as a gift.

'Is it a family matter, Delia?' she asks. Her eyes are cool, offering conventional politeness.

'Yes.' I smile at her. 'My father died tomorrow.'

Pink, black and silver. I designed our suite of offices before Lal joined us. Every room but mine has glass walls and mirrors so that there is an illusion of vast floating space in what is actually a small area. In the foyer near the elevators, black flamingoes and silver palms decorate a pink marble pool with a fountain. At one time, the fountain was barely audible. The first thing Lal did was to change the flow so that the water now pings precisely on a series of small bronze drums. The effect charms clients but drives new reception- ists mad until they manage selective deafness.

Sylvie makes coffee and we sit at the conference table, Sylvie, myself, Mark, Antwan, Philippa, Momo and Aaron, going through the schedule for the next week. Lal is in Poughkeepsie today and won't be back until the late train.

'You want I should call him?' Mark offers. He is a gifted wood designer and in love with Lal. He suffers deeply. I sometimes wonder why he torments himself by working in this place although I suppose if you can't have the pleasure of love, the pain is better than nothing.

'Thanks, Mark, but I left a message already on his voice mail. Now, the Brewster contract. The lighting is all concealed except for the Tiffany in the lounge.'

'Tiffany?' Philippa screws up her mouth and nose into a yeech.

'The client is always right, darling,' says Mark. 'Delia, I'll try him again. I just know he would want to be here with you.'

'Sure,' agrees Sylvie. 'It'd be number one priority. The Poughkeepsie job's in the bag anyway.'

I shush them. 'It's not exactly a personal tragedy. He's been bedridden for nearly six years.'

'When did you last see him?' Aaron asks.

'Two. Two and a half years ago. I stopped off on my way to Cape Town. Remember we were all big on Africana? Fetish dolls, and bamboo chairs?'

'Elephant shit incense,' says Aaron. 'Everyone wanted their apartment to look like a game reserve.'

'I was in New Zealand for a couple of days. I thought then he wouldn't last more than a month. It's too bad when you want to die and you've got a heart like a Pratt and Whitney engine.'

'Why sure, Delia,' says Antwan. 'It might be a blessing and all for him, but it's still a loss for the rest of you. Your sister's a restaurateur in Wellington New Zealand, right? You got other family?' Antwan is the firm's expert on family trivia. He heads a team of painters and paper-hangers and knows all their birthdays, the ages of their children, the status of their parents. It's a hobby that says much about his generosity but I frequently find it invasive.

'Beatrice has a married son Francis. The Munros are not known for prolific breeding. Now, where were we?'

'I was going to call Lal,' says Mark, half-rising.

Momo taps her pen on the table. 'The Brewster's Tiffany lamp.'

'Right!' I say. 'It should be in Foss and Hillman's new shipment of Mexican stained glass. Philippa, will you check that? Now, the marble for the lobby of the brownstone on 34th. The samples were the wrong colour. Someone has to go down and sort this out. Don't listen to any old hard-luck story. It's a big job. If they haven't got it, we go elsewhere. Sylvie, will you –'

'No, I won't!' Sylvie pushes back her chair. 'Delia, it's

past five and we've got a home to go to. Don't worry! We're all big boys and girls and you're away six days, not six months.

I look at the faces around the table and realise that I've been talking to them the way I talk to Beatrice. Do we ever grow beyond the relationships of childhood? I close my planner and laugh. 'I love you guys!'

51st Street between 2nd and 3rd is a narrow aorta clogged with traffic, garbage, chained bicycles, construction materials, illegally parked vehicles and jostling umbrellas. Under a wet awning, buckets of flowers do heroic battle with street smells. Pizza is spilled over the sidewalk. The subway breathes into the street and car exhausts throb the grey smoke of impatience.

It was a long dying, Dad. What did you have to learn from it? Acceptance? Fortitude? Surely, they were already yours.

In a doorway, someone is sleeping under a tent of cardboard and plastic. Only the feet are seen, wrinkled socks, worn slip-ons of an indefinable colour resting on an open newspaper. A blue neon sign blinks Tarot Readings, Palmistry and ESP, the Answer to all Your Problems. Further along, outside the Pickwick Arms Hotel, Lubov is pounding his hands, shaking his grey head like a dog. 'Wo Delia! You look friz, gal. How come you ain't got no coat?' Past the steamed windows of the café and the smell of wet pigeon droppings, I see a styrofoam cup wobbling down the flooded gutter. It becomes stranded on a grating as the water falls away.

That's the human condition, a styrofoam cup to be filled, emptied, filled, emptied, filled again, and constant confusion between container and content. Not that it matters. I expect that it's all part of the one comic cosmic concerto.

Lal says that one day there'll be computer programmes

that will analyse the energy vibrations of matter and convert the unheard sound of things to audible music. An interior decorator will be able to compose a kitchen or bedroom like a concerto or nocturne, selecting the right vibrations for the occupier so that we will all be able to live in chosen harmony with our surroundings. I like the idea but doubt its practical application. Lal's great gift is contagious beauty. He is not the most practical of beings. Still, I warm towards his notion that we subconsciously choose an environment that is sympathetic to our personal energy field. I know the symphony of this street just as surely as Beethoven heard the music of the moon. I know the fortissimo of the ambulance, the mezzo-forte of the garbage truck, the leggiero of pigeon wings and sniffing dogs, the glissando of falling leaves. I know the brass, the woodwinds, the timpani of traffic, the heavier percussion of the subway, the violin and cello voices of the sidewalk, the harp-playing morning sunlight between the trees in the Greenacre Park. The street fills me with the richest music and when I am away from it for any time, I hunger.

'Listen to your mother,' Dad used to say. 'I never had a chance to learn music and look at me, missed out.'

No, Dad, I don't think you did miss out. She worshipped music and we all envied her but you know, it is not possible to make a god of something without making a demon also.

I walk over the wet newspaper blown against the step and push open the glass doors, say, 'Hi!' to Rex the doorman who sits on the corner of his desk eating a hamburger. He oomphs at me, his mouth too full for conversation. What was the profound thought that I brought in out of the rain? Oh yes, gods and demons. You could say that was the problem with music, or poetry, or any of the arts. Once you opened the door to beauty you lived in a haunted house forever.

You, Dad, you worshipped her.

The elevator is an old and predictable friend that starts with as much effort as an invalid getting out of a chair. It shudders. Its cables creak. It whines and groans out the sad story of its day. Then it lurches to a stop on the fourth floor and trembles with the effort of opening its doors, reminding me once again of its martyred existence. In a corner of the elevator is a list of the signatures of attendants who have checked and serviced it. The last person signed, King Kong.

I turn the key in the lock which also creaks. Lal says the building went up circa 1930. Clever lady that Circa. Lived for centuries and created houses, poetry, music, always signing with the date. I told Lal that Circa's equally famous twin brother designed political systems and never signed his name. But what made me think of that? Oh shoot, I'm tired.

Our apartment is in darkness, warm, scented with garlic and ginger and lemongrass, and I realise that Lal must have prepared supper before he went to Poughkeepsie this morning. I turn a light on. There's the head of an aubergine in the sink and some scraping of carrot, a few dry husks of garlic, a pot of water on the stove for the rice. I take off my wet jacket, drop it on the floor and check the phone for voice mail. Yes, yes, from Lal, two messages.

'Delia, sweetheart, there's an aubergine curry in the fridge. If you want you can grill yourself some chicken as well. I'll do the rice and breads when I get there. I expect to be in by nine.'

The second is in a different voice.

'Delia, I have your news, sweetheart, and I am so very sorry. I'll finish these specifications as soon as I can and try for an earlier train. I forgot to mention there's some of your favourite dessert, mango kulfi, in the icebox.'

I erase the messages. Lal knows me. He doesn't have to put on the mask of tragedy or placate me with sweetmeats. I

17

go through the apartment switching on every light and put some Purcell loud on the CD player. Ta-rum, ta-rum. Ta-ra, ta-ra. Trumpets bounce spitballs off the ceiling and walls and the maidenhair fern shivers, ta-ra, ta-ra, as I throw a suitcase on the bed. Why am I doing this? It's so pointless. There is still time to back out. Sorry, Bea, crisis at work, flights all booked, plane got hijacked. Sorry, Bea, but even the thought of going back to New Zealand bores me witless.

When Lal comes in he instantly reads my mood and gives me space. I wish he wouldn't. But he's right, of course. If he did try to console me I would push him away. Our conversation becomes a game of tennis between the kitchen and my bedroom.

I bat at him. 'I'm afraid Sylvie'll forget to phone Foss and Hillman on Friday morning. Then there's the marble. They sent the wrong samples.'

'Internet,' he lobs back. 'Or aren't they on-line in New Zealand?'

'Lal, remember that obsolete slogan – customer comes first? We let down one client and it'll go around like a forest fire.'

'Nothing's going to happen,' he says.

'That's what I'm afraid of.' I bellow. 'You'll all sit on your hands, godammit, and there is so much on right now. The timing is disastrous.'

He comes to the door, holding a wet spoon. The smell of curry follows him like a bridal train. His eyes reflect volumes but all he says is, 'You're upset, sweetheart.'

Upset? Well, ha-tiddly-ha, what an erudite observation. Upset as in spilled? Tipped over on my ear? Carefully, I close and lock my suitcase. 'Yes, I'm upset. I'm angry.' I drag the suitcase down to the floor. 'I don't know why I'm going. There's nothing I can do.'

'Come and eat,' Lal says.

'I don't want to eat.'

'You will.'

I follow him to the kitchen. 'There's only Beatrice. She and I have always been chalk and cheese. We don't even look alike.'

He nods over the table as he lights the candle. Oh-oh, candlelight. White damask cloth and napkins, silver servers. Bring out the handkerchiefs.

'Delia's last supper?' I ask.

He smiles and cups his hand around the match to blow it out. Then he goes to the counter and puts on the oven gloves. 'It's not surprising you have little in common.'

I shake my head. 'We've always been miles distant. She was this real whiny kid. She had dolls. I had my paints and pencils. She was fat. I was skinny. She was Dad's girl. I spent more time with Mum. All her life Bea got exactly what she wanted, only when she got it she didn't want it any more. She wanted what I had.'

He opens the oven. 'She probably admired you.'

'Lal, don't do this.'

'Some things are self-evident,' he says into the oven.

'You have never met Bea! You're making these facile judgments because you can't bear to be helpless when I have a problem. Actually you know zilch.'

'I know you are Scorpio and she is Gemini. That's a lot of energy to go wrong between you.'

'Energy? Oh! Choice coming from an Aquarian!' I stop, look again at the table and hit my head with my hands. 'Lal! It's your birthday!'

'You've had other things to think of,' he says.

'I'm sorry, Lal. Mea culpa. I grovel. I didn't even get you a present.'

He puts down a steaming dish of aubergines. 'One birthday's much like another, so long as there are plenty of them. Your father wouldn't have wanted any more.' He goes back for a bowl of dhal, another of yoghurt and a stack of naan breads.

'It's not Dad's death that made me forget. I feel awful.'

He fills our glasses. 'Good,' he says, 'go on feeling awful. You forgot last year too. But okay, sweetheart, I'll survive.'

'I'll bring you a gift from New Zealand.'

He laughs. 'A T-shirt with sheep.'

I love his laughter and the way it shapes his face. In our student days he looked too young to be handsome. His body had matured, leaving his face still in childhood, pink lips, rounded dimpled cheeks, huge eyes with lashes like spider's legs, straight baby hair that flopped when he ran. Now most of the hair and the plumpness has gone and his skin sits fine and smooth on his skull. The dimples have been lost in the lines between his nose and mouth, and his eyes, still large, are nested in deep sockets of blue and purple shadow. When he was young, his face moved a lot, every emotion on stage. Now it is much more still, like an autumn landscape of hills and hollows. When I look at him in this candlelight, I feel the contours as sleek as carved wood under my hand.

'So,' he says, 'you will have almost a week down there.'

'What are you getting at?'

'Nothing. Absolutely nothing. I was merely reflecting that other visits have been stopovers on the way to Sydney or Melbourne or Cape Town.'

'Leave it, will you, Lal?' I raise my glass. 'Happy birthday.'

'Thank you. You really don't want to talk about it?'

'No.' I nod towards the CD player. 'Let's play something else. I'm sick of Purcell.'

Hours later, I am lying in bed, listening to distant sirens, when I begin to shake. It happens for no reason. The emptiness within me becomes charged with an electricity that sets my arms and legs going like the old elevator. I feel no grief, no loss and now, no anger, yet even my teeth are rattling like hailstones. I get out of bed and go to Lal's room.

'Lal, are you awake?'

'Yes?'

'Can I sleep with you?'

He has already moved over and pulled back the covers. 'You're very cold,' he says, putting his arms around me.

'I know.'

'You're not getting sick, sweetheart?'

'No.' Already the warmth of him is easing through my nightshirt, my skin, the muscles in spasm. Something inside me that has been like a fist all day begins to relax and open.

He strokes my hair. 'You are so unlike my mother.'

I smile that he should even compare us at this moment and rest my cheek against his shoulder. He never wears pyjamas. His skin is smooth and almost hairless and he smells of neroli oil.

'You see how she wails and weeps gallons and then there's an end of the matter, a true vata personality. You are such a pitta person, all that fire and you hold it in until it burns a hole in you.' He laughs gently. 'That is why you're freezing. Do you want to stay here the night?'

'Yes. May I?'

'Of course.' His hand still on my hair. 'Do you want anything?'

I shake my head. 'Just hold me Lal.'

'Talk or sleep?' he asks.

'Sleep,' I say and then I tell him how my office filled up with Dad.

2
BEATRICE

I know I'm old when I want to call a priest, son. It's Father
O'Donnell's curate Father Paul, such a lovely boy, with apple
pink cheeks and a smile you could serve up for lunch. He
brings me a cup of tea, half of it in the saucer, and offers me
some bought biscuits in a tin. Gingernut and milk arrowroot.
What a shame. Doesn't anybody bake for them? I take one
though, to keep the smile, and see his hands soft as bread
dough, the fingers long, a perfect almond nail on each, white
against the black trousers hanging low on his hips. He goes
on smiling, smiling because he thinks I'm thinking bereave-
ment and because they told him in the seminary that old
women are safe. Don't you believe it, son. Bless me Father, I
have sinned. There was this joke, you know. Two men stand
in the fires of hell and one is saying to the other, 'Unfortunately, mine were all sins of omission.' Move away, there's a
good lad. Never stand like that in front of a seated woman
even if she's as old as your grandmother, which she isn't, and
here he comes, Father Fion, as dry as an old crust, and that's
an end to it. The boy puts the lid on the biscuit tin and
swings his lovely hips, innocent as milk-fed veal, out of the
room, still smiling, bless his heart. We are back to funerals.

Father Fion O'Donnell is thin and stooped. The bones of his back show through his shirt, making a row of cotton reels and two budding wings. He walks with his elbows out wide and sharp. His glasses are always falling down his nose and he pokes them back up by the lenses which are permanently smeared with fingerprints. He folds himself into an armchair, looks at his notes, says, 'Would Delia want to do a reading?'

'I don't think so. She's not –'

'What about you, Beatrice?'

I consider it. 'No, Father, I don't think I could.'

'Tears are a gift,' he says.

I shake my head. 'Maybe Frank will. Francis. My son.'

'I thought we might move away from a traditional reading and look at the first letter of St John, chapter 4. Some beautiful verses, there are, on love. As I've said so often, what really impressed me about your parents was the way they kept their love alive and romantic even in their older years. I would see them coming up the church steps on a Sunday morning, and it was something to behold, the way they looked out for each other. They'd be clasping hands and he would have his other hand under her elbow and their gaze would be connected with this wonderful light of pure love.'

I'm nodding, yes Father, but thinking they were just scared of falling down the steps. Mum had osteoporosis and Dad had broken an ankle when he was mowing the lawns that time. But yes, a reading on love would be appropriate.

'I scarcely ever saw one on their own. Always a couple. They put me in mind of an old Sufi saying, God created man and woman from the one soul. That's not Church teaching, mind you. It's poetry. But I couldn't help feeling that when your mother died sudden like that, your father's soul was so entwined with hers that she took most of it with her. These last years have been a terrible trial for him. And for you,

Beatrice, driving up from Wellington every weekend.'

'Not every weekend, Father. Not quite.'

'In the mystery of eternal life, I'm certain they're together. You'd have to say that was God's plan, wouldn't you think? You know, sometimes you look at a man and you know his future's in commerce or teaching or farming or maybe the church, but you don't often think of a man having marriage as a true vocation.'

Why not, Father? Why the heck not? But I don't say anything because he will laugh and flick the words away with his hand and tell me he's too old for feminist politics. That's the way it is. The tea in my saucer slops onto my skirt. 'Yes, they were always lovers.'

'I want to say something about that in my homily. Your parents shared something marvellous that restored people's faith in marriage and in themselves. It meant a lot to me personally. Celibacy is a sacrifice. If marriage means nothing, you know, then the sacrifice is belittled.'

I am wondering how long it will take him to remember that I have had two marriages, three long-term de facto relationships and enough affairs to make the *Guinness Book of Records*. I put my cup and saucer down on the table. 'I'll leave it all to you, Father.'

'And I thought I'd mention your mother's last words to him. How he was working away in the shed and she just popped in to tell him she loved him on the way to get the mail and then her heart gave out down by the gate and she went to God just like that with the words of love still on her lips.'

Really! Was it like that? I don't think so but I can't take it away from him. I smile and nod.

'You're happy with the hymns?' he asks.

'Oh yes.'

'We'll have the piano music before the Mass. What a pity you don't have her own tape but never mind, it's the one she used to play for him, even if it's another pianist. Beethoven's Moonlight Sonata. Lovely thing. Never get tired of it. When is your sister arriving?'

But I can't answer. Suddenly, I am full of tears.

A pregnant woman should not wear heels that high. And why is she in black? Frank too. Well, not quite. Dark navy, white shirt, tie in navy, white and red diagonal stripes and his father's jaw, oh yes, Barry's great nutcracker jawbone out there slaying the Philistines. Frank. Francis. He hasn't got the same gift of the gab as his father, who could sell shit wrapped in cellophane, but the jaw is there. The mouth is neither Barry's nor mine. It's thin and wide, the same as Mum's and Delia's.

Spiky heels pick their way across the gravel and she says, 'Did we make an appointment?'

'You can visit any time,' I tell her.

'What Chloe means,' says Francis, 'is that they have a viewing room and they bring the – the departed out. You need to give them some warning.'

I know what Chloe means. 'They're expecting us,' I say firmly. But it's a lie, a lie, mud in your eye. We have to wait in a room of red carpet, blue satin chairs, masses of silk flowers, while they get him. Get him ready. There is music playing, something half sacred, half secular, tinkled out on a glocken-spiel. Actually, I think it's a dulcimer. The air is thick with the kind of perfume that gets sprayed out of cans.

'It's like waiting your turn in a brothel,' I say.

Francis has some kind of muscular spasm and his face sets, but his wife doesn't even flicker. She is very neat, nothing frayed or creased. Francis, too, for that matter.

Always has been. Shoes shining, socks unwrinkled, laces done up just so. When he stayed on the farm he cried when he got sheep muck on his knees. He was eight years old, too. Where did he get that for heaven's sake?

Mr Bulson opens the door and invites us into the viewing room. He is not an undertaker but a funeral director and it's not a coffin but a casket and my breath goes because he, because Dad. Lying there, so young. His skin is smooth, glossy with living colour. His lips are closed, almost smiling and his cheeks are full. The grey suit he hasn't worn for years fits neatly at the shoulders. His knobbly hands are folded, thumbs interlocked, over the second button of the jacket. He looks so pleased, so real, so.

'They must have found his teeth,' I say to Frank.

'Cosmetics,' says Chloe.

'Well now,' says Frank. 'Well, now, Grandpa.' He puts his hands behind his back and rocks on his toes. 'He's just the way I remember him.'

'They pad the cheeks,' Chloe says.

Oh Dad! Tears are coming again. I lean over quickly and kiss him on the forehead. His skin is cold and not quite hard, like wax fruit. Oh Dad, Dad, Dad, Dad, Dad.

Frank takes my arm and draws me away. 'Come on, Mother. Let's go back to the motel.'

As I step back, Chloe moves up to the coffin and makes the sign of the cross with her thumb on his forehead. How can she do that? She never really knew him. Frank puts his arm around my shoulders and offers me his handkerchief. 'You wouldn't want him back,' he says.

I go out to the car, mopping my face and wondering how many people have said those exact words? All of them, I think. You wouldn't want him back, blah-blah. It's a blessed release, blah-blah. He had a good life. Why doesn't someone just come out with, 'Hear your father dropped off his perch and you're feeling bloody awful.' Not likely. Life is full of clichés, especially at the end. That's the way it is.

As we drive to the motel, Chloe says, 'Did Francis tell you about the client from New York?'

'His suit looked nice,' I say. 'You know the last time he wore it was to Grandma's funeral?'

Frank laughs. 'Mother, you won't believe this. How many million people in Manhattan? This bloke is relocating to Sydney and he tells me that the New York apartment he just sold was completely redesigned and redecorated by Delia Munro.'

'Isn't it a small world?' says Chloe.

'He says she's got a great reputation. Last year there was half a page in the *Sunday Times*.'

'He couldn't believe that Francis was her nephew,' Chloe says.

'The sous-chef at Kiwiana,' I tell them. 'Julia's her name. She used to work at a restaurant in Auckland owned by someone very famous. Worth billions. He kicked the bucket. Heart attack. And the family bought him this elegant designer suit to lay him out in. Pure silk and alpaca. Thousands of dollars worth. Well, the undertakers didn't screw the lid of the coffin down properly and coming out of the church.' I start wheezing with laughter. 'Coming out of the church one of the pall-bearers stumbles. The coffin gets dropped and the tycoon rolls out. He's wrapped in newspaper!'

Frank looks at me.

'Plain newspaper! The undertakers had flogged the suit. The family wouldn't have found out if. If they'd have.'

'Sounds like one of those urban myths,' says Frank.

'It's true. It actually happened.'

'Stories like that abound,' he says.

'This, Frank, is gospel. Ask Julie. She'll tell you. There was a court case and.'

Neither of them speaks. After a while, Chloe says, 'We're hoping now you've got more time you'll come to Sydney. The children would like to see you again, Beatrice.'

'You're welcome to stay with us,' says Francis.

'After the baby's born,' Chloe says.

'Thank you.' Lie, lie. 'I would like that.'

We pull up outside the motel and I go into the office for their key while Frank pulls the bags out of the car.

The man in the office is called Billy. That's what he said yesterday, 'Billy rhyming with Willy,' flicking his eyebrows at me. He is thirty maybe, thirty-five, these days they all look impossibly young, and is sweetly running to fat. There are fleshy gaps between the buttons of his shirt and a pinch-size roll under his chin.

'Gooday, love,' he says. Three days of eye talk and he has moved to a new familiarity. Oh, he can pick them, all right.

'The key for 208. My son and his wife. You remember I booked the adjacent unit for them?'

He picks a key from a board. 'Never!' he says, dangling it between his fingers.

'I spoke to you about it yesterday morning.'

'Never you got a married son,' he grins as he leans across the counter, and down the neck hole of his shirt I see a gold chain dangling in a lawn of black hair. Men make such a fuss of women's chests. Do they realise that women feel the same about theirs?

I snatch at the key, my eyes meeting his, clash, clash, as he pulls it back out of reach. 'He's older than you,' I say.

He laughs, his breath sweet with gum and presses the key warmly into my hand. 'I always reckon women age like wine.

Some turns to vinegar but others get to be so –' He looks over my shoulder and his face goes blank.

'Have you got the key, Mother?' says the voice behind me.

Saint bloody Francis.

3
1953

For the rest of her life Delia would remember it as a day of gold. The images, the feeling, even the sky turned gold in her memory, although in fact the sky was blue and it was the plane in it that was as yellow as a buttercup. The music was definitely golden, a Chopin waltz that ran up and down Midas keys and her mother, bent over the keyboard, was wriggling her shoulders and head the way she did when she got full of the piece she was playing. Memory said, golden mother, golden fingers, golden light on the floor and the lid of the piano, golden sunflowers at the window, summer golden grass and golden fire dropping out of the sky. Actually, it wasn't like that. Delia didn't hear the plane, partly because of the piano and partly because she was at the kitchen table, deeply occupied with a coloured pencil drawing of a medieval castle for a school project. It was Bea who came running in yelling, 'Uncle Jack's here! Uncle Jack! Uncle Jack!'

The piano stopped, the pencil fell onto the table and the house trembled with a noise of the aeroplane engine which sounded like Mum's old sewing machine with the pedal flat down. Delia pushed her chair back. 'Mum, it's Uncle Jack.'

Her mother's back was straight with listening but she didn't turn around or speak. The machine vibrations stitched up all the air in the room so that they were breathing it in and it was growing in them like another heartbeat.

'Mum?' Delia smiled at the back of her mother's head, willing her to be pleased.

The spine stayed as stiff as iron but the hands went back to the piano keys. It was the Chopin waltz again, fast and very loud.

They ran out, Delia, Bea, tripping over the gumboots in the back porch, pushing each other, stumbling down the path to the woolshed, their heads tilted to the sky, hands waving, waving, oh Uncle Jack, can you see us?

The yellow Tiger Moth was circling low over the house, the black letters under its wings as big as newspaper headlines, ZK-BFA, and he saw them all right. The round head of the flying helmet was nodding, the goggles glinting, a hand waving hello to the scallywags, the ratbags, the honey pies, the niftiest girls in the world, and then the yellow wings tipped the other way, heading for the paddock where Dad had cleared a landing strip. They chased after it, Bea puffing because her legs were short, and climbed onto the barbed wire fence by the orange windsock that hung like an elephant's trunk. 'Uncle Jack! Uncle Jack!' Each shielded her eyes with her left hand and waved with her right, yelling, although he would not have heard a thing.

The aeroplane waggled its wings in the sun, turned, then dropped down towards them, angled so that they could clearly see him in the rear cockpit, goggles like beetle's eyes and his big-teeth grin and the leather jacket that he had let Delia wear, with half the sleeves flapping over her hands. Down it came, the golden noise of it washing over them and then suddenly the feeling of it was too much for Delia. She brought her right hand down on a barb on the top wire and closed her fist until the pain took over.

The wheels touched the grass, bounced a little and then the tail skid came down. The aeroplane taxied almost to the end of the paddock and turned around, trundling back to them. It blew a rush of dust and straw in their faces and they backed off the fence, coughing and wiping their eyes.

Uncle Jack didn't put down the little gate of his cockpit but jumped over it, one hand on the back of the seat, and in a second had flicked open the luggage space behind him, taking from it two triangular blocks of wood with ropes hanging off them. In the same quick way, he wedged the wood under the wheels. The Tiger Moth chugged quietly against them, its wings trembling, its propeller making a slow circle of light.

He came to them, pulling off his gloves and lifting his goggles up on his helmet. Delia saw the fizzy blue of his eyes framed by the deep marks left by the goggles.

'Hi sugar!' He put his hand on Delia's head. 'Hi Buzzy Bea!' The other hand rested on Bea's plaits. 'Where's my pal Frankie?'

'Back up the hill!' Bea shouted. 'He's got fly strike!'

Delia put her hand on Bea's arm to silence her. 'It's the hot weather. The blowflies have been bothering the sheep. He's got the motorbike. He probably saw you coming.'

'He paints flyspray stuff on sheeps' bums,' shouted Bea, laughing and squirming.

Delia glared at her. Bea always did this kind of thing to get attention. She was nine, old enough to know better.

'What say we go and look for him,' laughed Uncle Jack. 'Anyone want a ride?'

'Me, me, me!' Bea was trying to get her chubby leg over the fence but her dress got caught on a barb.

'Delia first because she's the oldest,' said Uncle Jack, lifting Delia over the fence as easy as can be. As he set her on the ground he grabbed her right hand and opened it to look at the blue and red hole in the middle of her palm. She would have to lie about that. How could she explain that when a big feeling hurt her she had to find another hurt to take her mind off it? But she didn't need to say anything. Before he could ask the question in his eyes, Bea was bawling and saying, 'It's not fair! It's not fair!'

'You'll be second, honey bun,' he said.

'I saw you first,' sobbed Bea. 'Delia was inside and she didn't even –'

'No blubbering near my Tiger. It rusts the instruments.' He unbuttoned his leather jacket, shrugged it off and draped it around Bea's shoulders. The weight of it brought her down from the fence and she stood on the grass, shoulders bent, her wet face glowing.

'Keep it warm for me, my little Buzzy Bea. We'll be back pronto.'

He was wearing a white nylon shirt that flapped in the wind from the propeller and Delia could see the gingery hairs on his chest as he strapped her into the front cockpit. He tightened the cross of canvas webbing across her chest. 'That feel okey-doke?' he yelled. 'You sure you're going to be warm enough? It's cold up there.'

She nodded. She was trembling, though not with cold. She had never been in an aeroplane before but couldn't tell him that lest he think her too much of a kid and change his mind. She looked at the dials, the pedals at her feet, the black stick with the knob a little above her knees. It was called a joystick. She knew that from reading *Biggles* books.

He followed her gaze. 'It's a trainer,' he said. 'Kitted out for dual. Hold your mouth the right way and I might let you fly it. How old did you say you were?'

'Twelve.'

'Nah,' he laughed. 'Not a day under twenty-one. Come on, let's see if the helmet fits you.'

It was almost the same as his, a leather hat with lambs-wool inside, goggles sitting on top, a strap with a buckle and a tube like a doctor's stethoscope hanging from the ear things.

'This is a Gosport tube. I'll plug this in and you'll hear me from the back cockpit. You want to talk to me, just yell here. Okay? Okay! Don't touch anything until I tell you.' He did the helmet up under her chin and pulled the goggles down over her eyes. They were made of perspex and a little scratched but she could see through them fine. She lifted her hand to wave to Bea but only her fingertips moved. He tugged again at the harness and then put up the hatch, the little gate into the cockpit with two bolts to keep it in place.

Delia sat up straight and looked at everything, the yellow wings above and below, the struts, the wires, the bulge of the petrol tank, the propeller that whirred wind into her face and hair. Uncle Jack was pulling away the triangular chocks. It was going to happen. She was going to fly.

A lever at her side moved forward, the engine roared and the aeroplane shook like a startled horse. Slowly it turned around and rolled across the paddock, bumping towards the place where it had landed. The sun was in her eyes, splintered by scratches in the goggles, chopped up by the propeller. The dry summer hills shimmered into liquid shapes that flowed around her, hurting with their beauty. She clenched her hands in her lap and saw it all, the knobs and levers that shifted by themselves, the lichen on the fence-posts, Beatrice sitting in the yellow grass with the jacket over her knees, the elephant's trunk barely moving. Uncle Jack's voice, stretched out thin by the tube, said in her ears, 'Trim okay, mixture back rich, fuel okay, ignition, harness and hatches. Final cockpit check done, sugar puss. Are you ready?'

She nodded.

'You okay up there?'

'Yes, YES!' she yelled.

'Here we go, kiddo.'

The engine grew louder, the wheels faster, the bumps bigger. They roared past Bea who was waving both arms and Mum who was running to the fence, waving, and then the knob between Delia's knees moved back into the hem of her dress, the joystick, and the bumps had gone and the wheels were off the ground. They were in the air.

She held her hands so tight that the pain from the barbed wire went right up her arm and became a part of her laughter. The fences were falling away, the house, the wool-shed, the tractor like a little brown toy. The sky shifted sideways and they were flying back over the strip. Beatrice and Mum together at the fence, small as insects under the orange splash of the windsock and there was a different kind of bumping, the wings bouncing in the bright golden air.

'How'd you like that, sugar puss?'

'I love it! I just love it!'

His laugh was warm in the helmet. 'Okay. Now let's look for Frankie Munro. Did they ever tell you I was their best man?'

'Yes!'

'He's beaut. A real corker, your Dad.'

'Yes.' She looked down at a lumpy mattress of hills, burned yellow and blue with shadow in the creases, and the clusters of sheep as small as maggots. The wind whipped her hair against her goggles. The plane bucked and shivered, making her stomach drop.

'Thermals,' he said. 'It's the heat. You get uneven air like potholes in a road.'

'I can see our shadow!' she yelled. It was underneath them, a dark plane shape sailing over the hills.

'You know how fast we're travelling? Look at the gauge in front of you. Forty-eight miles per hour cruising speed, altitude 1100 feet and climbing. Can you spot your Dad?'

She tried to lean over the edge of the cockpit but the straps held her shoulders down. 'No.'

'Look to port!' he said and the joystick moved sideways. The wings tilted the other way and she saw a dark blob moving with smaller dark specks behind, her father on his motorbike, the dogs running after.

'He's not looking!' she yelled into the talking tube.

'He will. Want some fun?'

'Yes! Oh yes!'

They climbed into the sky in a slow spiral until the man on the motorbike was a tiny dot and the hills had shrunk to small ripples in a wider landscape of roads and houses rimmed by sea. The sun's glitter was fierce but there was no warmth and Delia's arms were blotched red and blue, pimpled below the sleeves of her cotton dress. The droning of the engine was even, like the buzzing of a big bumblebee, but they weren't going anywhere, just round and round with the nose pointing up and the propeller spinning away the blueness of the sky. After a long time, Uncle Jack levelled the plane and shouted in her ears, 'Right, kiddo, want to fly?'

She shook her head.

'Can you reach the rudders?' he said. 'Those are the bars by your feet.'

She looked down and was relieved to discover that her sandals barely touched the metal strips. 'No.'

'Don't worry. I'll do that bit. See the stick? Put your

hand on it and just do what I say. I'll tell you to pull it right back and then I'll tell you to push it forward. Ready?'

She nodded, her right hand over the black knob.

'Got it?' he said and she felt it waggle under her fingers.

'Yes.'

'Slowly pull it back, back. That's it. Back some more.'

She drew it towards her until the knob was almost in her lap. The aeroplane was rising up, nose in the air.

'Back until she stalls,' yelled Uncle Jack.

Suddenly, the engine cut out. The propeller slowed, stopped and the plane was sitting on its tail in a silent sky, the only noise the whistling of wind in the wires.

'Stick forward!' yelled Uncle Jack. 'Forward!' And already he had begun to push it for her. 'This is where the fun starts, kiddo.'

The plane's nose dropped until the brown hills were directly in front of her, then the line of the horizon tipped up and turned. She got a funny feeling in her stomach. Around the horizon went and around and around, the browns and blues mixing up like the colours of a spinning top and no sound at all but the wooshing of the wind. The pressure in her stomach grew bigger and pinned her into the seat. It was hard to breathe. Then the pedals in front of her feet moved and the stick flicked sideways in her hand and the horizon came back right side up. The engine started and all her insides floated down into their right places again. But her heart was slip-slopping in her ears and chest and hands and she was breathing fast as though she had been running.

'Like that?' yelled Uncle Jack.

'Yes!'

'We did a spin. Look down there.'

They were much closer to the ground now and she could see her father's red shirt, the way his gumboots were stuck out on either side of the motorbike, the dogs racing about barking. Dad was looking up and waving both arms, crossing them over his head. She put her arm out of the cockpit to wave back.

'Hold on, kiddo,' said Uncle Jack. 'We'll give him a little buzz.'

The engine bellowed and instantly the horizon tipped again. The earth was above her, the sky below. She gripped the edge of her seat as her haunches rose from it. The straps bit into her shoulders. She was hanging in them, hanging upside down. Uncle Jack was laughing in her ears. He swung the Tiger Moth over and she dropped back into her seat.

'That was a barrel roll,' he said. 'Want to bet old Frankie gets to the airstrip before we do?'

They were all at the airstrip, Dad, the dogs, Mum, Beatrice, and no one waved as the plane landed. Dad ran over, happy to see Uncle Jack. He climbed up on the wing and leaned over the back cockpit, punching Uncle Jack on the shoulder and yelling, 'Hell, Jack. What the blazes, Jack. Good to see you, you old villain.'

They shouted at each other while Uncle Jack ran down the engine and then Dad came to the front and unsnipped the hatch door. He took off Delia's harness, undid her helmet.

'Did you see the barrel roll, Dad?'

'I saw it,' he said but his smile was now so small it didn't count. 'You'd better go and see your mother.'

Uncle Jack's leather flying jacket was hanging over a fencepost. Delia would have liked to have wrapped it around her cold shoulders but she didn't care. They walked fast back to the house. Mum was holding Bea's hand and pulling her along whenever her snivelling slowed her down. 'He promised me!' Bea sobbed. 'It was my turn!'

Delia ran until she was ahead of them. She scuffed her sandals in the dry grass. 'I flew the plane,' she wanted to say. 'I flew it.' But that would only make things worse.

'What made you think you had the right?' her mother said to her back. 'You could have been killed.'

She didn't answer.

'I forbid you to ever go in that aeroplane again. Do you hear me, Delia? Delia?'

'Yes.'

Bea wailed, 'Uncle Jack promised me!'

'He is not your Uncle Jack,' her mother replied. 'He's your father's friend and that's it.'

'He's a good flier,' said Delia, flattening a clump of grass with her heel. 'I wouldn't have got killed. That's just stupid. Why can't we go in his plane?'

Her mother swept past her so fast that Bea was running. 'I don't have to give you a reason why, Delia.'

'Uncle Jack is our friend too,' she said.

'You girls have your own friends,' said her mother.

That was all she would say on the matter except to remind Delia from time to time that it was a wonder she wasn't killed. That prospect interested Bea who shut off her tears long enough to wonder what people looked like after they fell out of aeroplanes

'I expect they split open like watermelons,' Delia said.

Dad and Uncle Jack did not come down to the house until tea time. Delia saw them on the path, Uncle Jack's arm across Dad's shoulders, their heads bowed together in laughter. It looked to be a really big joke, yet by the time they got to the door, it had gone and they came in with separate quietness to wash their hands. Uncle Jack ran his hands through his hair to dry them and then tucked his shirt into his pants. He grinned at Mum, 'Aw, come on, lamb chop, it isn't the end of the world.'

She turned her back to him and spooned dressing over the salad.

'Aggie?' He tried again. 'Agnes?'

'Everyone sit down at the table,' she said.

Delia and Bea ran to their places, while Uncle Jack slowly shook his head. 'I got two thousand hours, Aggie. Just over two thousand friggin', sorry, hours. I know flying as well as you know that piano and nobody tells me I put kids' lives in danger.'

'We know that, Jack,' Dad said. 'Agnes was just a bit concerned because Delia went without permission.'

'She had my permission,' he said, slumping into a chair. 'Doesn't that count?' He leaned towards Mum who was carefully scraping out the salad dressing jug. 'Why don't you come for a spin, Aggie? Then you'd know. Safe as bloody houses, cross my heart and hope to die.'

'No thank you,' she said.

'Bloody great vote of confidence,' he said. 'Future instructor of the Middle District Flying School and she wouldn't trust me with a tricycle.' He reached across the table and stabbed cold mutton with his fork. 'This your own meat, Frankie?'

Dad said to Mum, 'Jack's got a job with the aero club in Palmerston North.'

'Oh?' Mum looked at Uncle Jack. 'You're not going back to Australia then?'

'Nah.' He shook the meat off his fork and onto his plate. 'Been offered a job as instructor. Bloody boring, excuse my French, but good enough pay. It's time I settled down like this old dingo.' He punched Dad on the arm. 'Find myself my own little lamb chop and breed a couple of scallywags.' He reached for the dish of boiled potatoes.

'Mum and me, we saw the plane falling down,' said Bea.

'You did not. A controlled spin from five and a half thousand feet and then a quick barrel roll. No falling down about it, Buzzy Bea.' He put a forkful of meat in his mouth.

'Who will bless the food?' Mum said.

He put down his fork. 'Sorry, I forgot. Better do a Jack grace. Two, four, six, eight. Bog in, don't wait.'

Beatrice sniggered and Delia kicked her under the table.

'Frank?' said Mum.

Dad crossed himself and raced through his usual slow blessing like Charlie Chaplin in a speeded-up movie. Then Mum passed around the salad, potatoes, cold meat. She had closed the windows to keep the flies out and the room was hot, the low sun firing straight in across the table.

Uncle Jack got talking about the war days when he and Dad were at the Rongotai air base together, Uncle Jack flying, Dad in the engineering workshops. It was a conversation about people Delia didn't know and parties and getting beer after the pubs were closed and Uncle Jack would say swearwords when he got excited. Mum was silent. Even if Uncle Jack said something terrible, she still wouldn't comment because he was Dad's best friend and it would show Dad up. But Delia knew that Mum would have something to say to Dad when Uncle Jack had gone and they were in the bedroom where the girls could not hear anything but a murmur through the walls.

After tea, Uncle Jack walked through to the living room and lifted the lid of the piano and poked a key with his forefinger. Mum, who was clearing the table, went still.

'How about a tune?' Uncle Jack called to her.

'I'm busy,' she said. 'Delia will play for you.'

'No!' Delia was filled with alarm. 'I can't. I'm just learning.'

Her mother said, 'Schumann's Melody, Delia. You play it very well.'

'No!' Delia backed away, ready to flee outside.

'Come on, Aggie,' Uncle Jack looked at Mum. 'One little tune and then you'll be rid of me, girl. Promise.'

Mum didn't answer but went on stacking dishes and Dad, not quite laughing, took the dishes from her hands and leaned his face against her hair. Maybe he was kissing her cheek. Maybe he was saying something. She wiped her hands on the dish towel and then ran them down the sides of her skirt as she went through to the piano. Uncle Jack stood back a bit as she sat down. She rubbed her hands together and rested her fingertips for a moment on the edge of the keyboard. He leaned against the piano, watching her.

She raised her hands and then brought them down on an uncomfortable chord. Delia had heard the music before. It was a Kabalevsky piece, full of sad slow notes, heavy and angular, offset by little arguing arpeggios that never quite connected. The sounds filled the long space that ran from kitchen to dining room to living room and became molten in the sunset. They reminded Delia of war and bombs and people crying.

Dad was watching Mum and smiling but Uncle Jack was tapping his fingers on the piano and shifting his feet. After two or three minutes, he said, 'That's enough!'

Mum stopped.

'You mean someone actually wrote that stuff?' he said. 'Shit a brick, girl, it's out of tune. Play something we can sing.' He clicked his fingers and did a few fancy steps around the piano. 'Crazy 'bout you, Baby. Sh-boom, sh-boom.

Now don't you tell me maybe. Sh–boom, sh–boom.'

Mum sat with her head bowed, her hands in her lap.

'You know "Sweet Violets"? "Ghost Riders in the Sky"?'

'I don't play that kind of music,' Mum said.

'Course you can. Frankie tells me you can play anything.'

Dad came forward, 'What about the "Moonlight Sonata"?' he said and Mum turned to him with a long look.

'Nah!' said Uncle Jack. 'None of that classical rubbish. An ordinary tune. Hey! If you want to do something fancy, what about "Black and White Rag"? You must know that. Winifred Atwell plays it. Dah–de–dah–de–dah–dah –'

Mum put down the piano lid and pushed back the stool. She stood up, her head still bent and said, 'I'm sorry. I've got things to do.' Then she walked back to the kitchen, her cheeks glowing red and her eyes bright with tears.

Uncle Jack said to Delia, 'Can you play "Black and White Rag"?'

'No! No!' Delia shook her head hard and went to the sink to help with the dishes.

'Ah well.' He looked up at the window and the setting sun. Then he checked his watch. 'I've got to get back, anyway.' He slapped Dad on the shoulder. 'Nice talking to me old mate again, and thanks for the tucker, Aggie. Tell you what. I'll see if I can find you the sheet music for "Black and White Rag". I bet you'd love it.'

Mum didn't look up from the dishes.

Beatrice grabbed Uncle Jack's wrist in both hands. 'When are you coming again, Uncle Jack?'

'Dunno, Buzzy Bea. Soon.'

She put her feet on his shoe and swung on his arm from side to side. 'Why don't you come with us when we go on holiday?'

He laughed. 'I'll have to think about that.'

'Think now,' she said. 'Now, now, now!'

'Bea!' said Delia. 'Mum, tell Bea to stop annoying Uncle Jack.'

'That's enough, Beatrice,' said Mum.

Delia wiped the tea towel around the inside of a cup and smiled up at him. 'Goodbye, Uncle Jack.' She noted the light in his fizzy blue eyes as he smiled back. 'Atta girl,' he said. 'Next time I need a co-pilot you'll be top of my list.'

They were cleaning up the last of the dishes when the Tiger Moth took off, circled once over the house and then flew towards Palmerston North. Long after the noise of its engine had gone, they saw it as small as a dragonfly heading straight into the sunset.

Dad was busy outside for a while, feeding the dogs and putting away the tools and the machinery. He came in just on dark and stood behind Mum who was reading at the table. He rubbed up and down her arms, crackling the material of her blouse with his rough farm hands and when she smiled at him and rested her head back, he bent over to kiss her.

Delia sat down at the piano. She had heard "Black and White Rag". It was played on the radio request sessions and her friend Susan had the record. Slowly, she picked out the melody with one hand. I-flew-the-plane-I-flew-the-plane-I-flew.

4
DELIA

Breakfast is finished and people are moving about the first-class compartment of the plane, involved in earnest conversations. It is too early in the day to be reshaping the world to fit personal preferences, especially with strangers. I close my eyes on a forthright opinion of the Asian economy and pretend to drift back to sleep. The man sighs, or perhaps I just imagine a sigh, and moves away as I rest my head against the window, using the endless space behind my eyelids as a screen for the old movies of memory.

Unfortunately, the movies are not endless, nor even plentiful. I am surprised by the amount I have forgotten. The latter half of my life has so eclipsed the first that I don't know who the old New Zealand self was. My childhood is like a part I once had in a play. I was the actress but not the author and now I can't remember any of my lines, although the stage sets are still so vivid that they dominate my dreams. I see the towns of Napier and Hastings as they were in the 1950s and 60s, the network of Hawke's Bay roads, the beaches, but mostly, I see the farm. In memory it is nearly always summer, and even when I am reconstructing winter with snow on the ranges and ice in the puddles, I am feeling summer warmth.

Frank and Agnes Munro are part of the stage set but I can't see clearly their faces, only their hands. Hers were very strong. The popular image of a pianist's hands suggests a long and delicate structure with expressive, beautifully tapered fingers. Mum's fingers were rather short and immensely sturdy. When you looked at them you thought, wire, and then wondered why. The pads of muscle on the backs of the hands and fingers rippled like biceps but that solid could turn to liquid on the keys, fingers moving so fast that they disappeared like some Leger painting into images of their own multiple vibrations. Dad's hands were strong too, but so different, big paws that had the stiffness of thick leather gloves. The slowness of his fingers on a washer or bolt could make you ache with impatience. He was slow in everything. You'd see him in the yards with hundreds of sheep bleating and churning, barking dogs running across woolly backs, the air filled with the smell of dust and dung and frenzy, and he would be moving in this sweet slowness as though he were counting sheep in a dream. He didn't talk much, not even to her. Looking back now, I realise that they were both quite inarticulate. They could make one or two sentences last an entire evening.

'Excuse me, Ms Munro. Excuse me.'

The steward is offering me a hot towel.

'Please, will you put the back of your seat up and stow your footrest for landing at Auckland airport?'

I glance at the window and am caught again by the loveliness of it, expected but always a surprise, such greenness, trees and paddocks sharp in the clear air, wet clouds, the white rim of sea. So much space. Houses spread out like tiny building blocks on a land that resonates with the power of the Saint-Saens organ symphony. That music always reminds me of this country, boom, boom, great chords of mountains, oceans, earthquakes and storms, and, perched on it, the grace notes of a little people. I look down and ache for the population's vulnerability.

'You been here before?' The man next to me snaps his seat belt.

I nod and turn from the window. 'Everything's so small.'

'Yeah.' He laughs. 'Makes you wonder what happens when the tide comes in.'

Lightheaded from sleep deprivation I check my luggage at the counter for the Napier flight and then wander through the airport looking for a card phone. When I finally get through to the office, I hear two bars of the Brandenburg Concerto and Philippa's voice, 'This is the office of Delia Munro and Associates, Decorators –'

'Philippa! It's Delia.'

'We are busy right now but we want you to know your call is important to us. Please leave a message after the tone and we'll get right back –'

I hang up and go to the gate for the Napier plane. It's not only jet-lag. I'm still carrying an emptiness that's as dense as a black hole. I can't name it but what's new? Life is full of the unnameable. It could be somehow connected with the stage set, and the way it has been dismantled piece by piece over the years. At one time I considered the farm to be a prison but even prisons become a part of us, absorbed by familiarity until they are a habit to our thinking. The farm buildings, the trees, those hills which were at one time an extension of ourselves, now belong to other lives and with Dad finally gone it seems there is nothing. Yes, I think the emptiness can be defined as a huge hole cut out of the map of belonging, but having said that I don't feel any better. Beatrice? Oh, she was never really a part of my personal landscape.

She is at the Napier airport, looking much the same as she was last visit, large in a sacklike dress, long frizzy hair going grey. Her face still has the roundness of childhood, round eyes, small round nose, lips as fat and round as two bee stings. 'Diddy!' she screams. 'Diddy! Over here!' Behind her is a well-presented young couple, a blonde woman in a cream dress and straw hat, the man standing square in a navy suit. Bea engulfs me, imprinting her heavy floral perfume and without meaning to, I back away from her eagerness and her unpleasant body heat. 'Diddy, you know Francis?' she says.

'Why hello, Francis.' I am truly surprised. 'Just look at you. I haven't seen you since – when? Your grandmother's funeral?'

'I didn't get over for that,' he said. 'The last time I saw you, Mother took me to Disneyland and you met us in Los Angeles. Aunt Delia, this is my wife Chloe.'

'Chloe. It's so nice to meet you at last.' I take her hand. She is a smiling young woman with cool quick eyes and a pregnant bulge in her dress. 'Now let me get this right. You and Francis have two children?'

Bea says, 'Three. They have two boys and a girl. The youngest girl is very good on the piano.'

Chloe places her hand on her abdomen. 'Three and a half,' she says. 'May I call you Aunt Delia? I'm dying to hear about your work.'

'Just Delia, please.' I try to move. We are standing in a stream of arriving passengers and the noise of flight announcements.

'Plenty of time for talk over lunch,' says Bea, grabbing my arm and steering me towards the exit. 'We're going to a nice restaurant on the Esplanade and then we'll take you back to the motel to unpack. You and I are sharing a unit but it's got two bedrooms. Will that be all right? Oh

Diddy, it's wonderful having you back home.'

'Sure, Bea. Do you mind if I get my luggage first?'

She laughs and puts her hand over her mouth. 'Of course! I meant that. You've got such an accent, Diddy. Doesn't she sound American, Frank?'

My clothing still smells of stale aircraft and my eyes feel full of grit. There's nothing I want more than a shower and a nap. I also need to phone Lal. But the luncheon has been planned and I don't have the energy to run against Bea's enthusiasm. As we drive from the airport she tries to bring me up to date with New Zealand politics while Francis and Chloe slide under her voice with questions about my work.

'Did you really redecorate a house for Robert Kennedy?' Chloe asks. 'What about the Welsch building? Was that your firm?'

'Where do you advertise?' says Francis.

'Francis is a land agent,' says Bea. 'He's got an office in Forrest Hills. That's near Sydney. A very busy area with absolutely beautiful homes.'

'A realtor,' Chloe says.

I always forget how bright the light is here, how the sun throws itself against every surface so that the eyes are being constantly fire-bombed. Within minutes I feel as though I've suffered an entire fourth of July fireworks display and I can't find my shades.

'This ex-New Yorker,' says Francis, 'he told me you had such a reputation that you didn't have to advertise. People came to you and you could pick and choose, he said.'

'Don't you believe it.' I close my eyes. 'Excuse me. I've had planes and airports for some thirty hours.'

That doesn't stop them. Their voices blend in a verbal soup and I wonder at the texture, the slowness and flatness of the vowels. Perhaps I do have an accent, after all. Ah, here they are, at the bottom of my pocket-book, my bifocals with the photo-chromatic lenses.

Napier surprises me with its freshness, an art deco city in bright colours that leap out at me like a Warner Brothers cartoon. Has it all been painted? I seem to recall a black-and-white town crumbling at the edges but perhaps my fogged mind is mixing childhood memory with the old newspaper clippings of the great Napier 1931 earthquake. At school, we thought the pictures of smashed buildings and bodies gave us the edge over other New Zealand towns and put us on a world map with San Francisco and towns in Japan, Alaska, Peru. The teacher's dissertation on earthquakes left blanks which our fertile minds quickly filled. We saw the tectonic plates of the Pacific rim as great blue-and-white dishes sliding over each other in soapy water, cracking, breaking, causing tidal waves in the sink. For whatever reason, Napier had been chosen, not for tragedy as we saw it, but for fame. When Sister Marcella took us into the church to light a candle and pray for the souls of the victims, one of them being her father someone discovered, we felt a fine importance as we knelt in our gym tunics in front of the calm statue of Mary.

'You'll see a lot of changes,' Beatrice says. 'The town and the foreshore. It's really quite attractive.'

'I was thinking of the earthquake. Do you remember how possessive we felt about that? How mad we got with that Wellington girl who told us Wellington would never have a fatal earthquake because the Archbishop had placed it under the protection of Mary?'

She frowns in concentration. 'No,' she says, 'no, I don't remember that. Dad loved Napier. I think he would have moved into town if Mum had been more social. That's the restaurant up ahead. Lovely views. We thought your tongue would be hanging out for some real New Zealand seafood and real New Zealand wine.'

I stop myself from telling her that we can get both in New York and I feel the lion rampant of irritation slowly subside until it's on four paws again. Why do I let her get to me like this?

I am not hungry but I pick over some grilled blue cod and a glass of an excellent chardonnay. The views are truly lovely, white sand, blue sea, gulls drifting like scraps of paper and the sweep of the Napier foreshore like some Dufy painting of the French Riviera. Although I guess that if Dufy had been here he would not have painted it in the same way. The thick sweeps of his brush would have picked up the loneliness of it, the empty sky, empty sea, empty beach and over it all the harsh vacant light. Every time I come back I am struck by the loneliness of this country and the impermanence of the people who huddle on a land that belongs only to itself. It might be something to do with the lack of human history, only a thousand years, and the geographic isolation. Whatever, this earth does not wear the same veneer of human spirit that we touch in the countries of the Northern Hemisphere, and this salt-laden air is quite empty of ghosts.

'What do you think, Aunt Delia?' says Francis.

'Sorry –'

'Do you think Mother should expand? I reckon she should find a waterfront location in Auckland, something with this kind of ambience. The patrons would drive any distance for food of her quality. You don't get it these days. Low-fat is the excuse for low-taste. Nouvelle cuisine is the excuse for skimpy portions and cost-cutting.' He takes empty mussel shells from a bowl and places them on his plate. 'Kiwiana Wellington, Kiwiana Auckland and then, maybe, Kiwiana Christchurch.'

'Not at fifty-five,' laughs Bea. 'I dream of retiring, not expanding. For one thing, I'd like to spend more time with my grandchildren. Why don't you and Chloe come back? You could do it. We'd go into partnership. Is your cod all right, Diddy?'

'Oh yeah, it's great. It's just that I ate on the plane.'

'That was hours ago. The food here is good. Very fresh. I know you eat out a lot over there and I wouldn't have.'

'Why did you call your restaurant Kiwiana?'

'Because it's traditional kiwi food,' says Bea. 'I thought a long time on this. There was nothing wrong with the old kiwi dishes. It was just that we did such terrible things to. Sloppy cooking. If you come to Kiwiana and order steak and kidney pudding, you won't get grey meat and gravy in a soggy crust. Rump steak and ox kidney, sautéed with thyme, shallots, garlic, parsley, a little nutmeg and black pepper, the flavour deepened with sherry, steamed inside a soft suet pudding. And tripe. Remember the unspeakable tripe? You'll have to try it cooked in tomato juice with red peppers, corn, chilli, cumin, coriander –'

'It's a good name. What made you think of it?' I put down my fork. 'Kiwiana.'

'I didn't make it up.'

'You didn't?'

'Oh Diddy! You're so out of touch and I forget. We should phone each other more. With the cheap rates now there's no reason why we shouldn't talk at least once a week. Then you wouldn't.' She wipes her mouth with her napkin. 'Kiwiana is what we call all that old stuff, you know, the things you identify with New Zealand, like gumboots and Vegemite and –'

'Which is Australian,' says Francis.

'And the *Edmonds Cookery Book* and Aunt Daisy's handy hints and pavlova.'

'Pavlova also being Australian,' says Chloe.

'Hey!' I hold up my hands. 'Not the old pavlova argument.'

'Australia invented it,' says Chloe. 'To commemorate the Australian tour of the ballerina Pavlova in nineteen twenty something.'

'It was in a New Zealand cookbook two years before,' says Bea. 'That's been proved.'

I shake my head. 'And it was in French cookbooks a hundred years before that. Meringue gâteau. Only the name was changed.'

'So?' says Bea.

'It was an egg white dessert invented by the French,' I tell her.

'Kiwiana is New Zealand trivia,' says Francis. 'Wait until you see Mother's restaurant. It's decorated with all this amazing stuff which is symbolic of domestic New Zealand. Railway posters. Yates Seeds packets, that kid's toy Buzzy Bee, black woollen bush singlets, paua shell –'

'Black woollen bush singlets? Good God, Bea, you actually make an icon of bush singlets in a restaurant?'

Francis points his solid jaw at me. 'It's a down-under thing, Aunt Delia. Like the Aussies and their swagger hats with the hanging corks.'

'I understand.' I fold my napkin, or I should say, serviette. 'The wine and fish were excellent, Bea. Thank you. Are we proceeding to the motel?'

She leans across the table. 'Let me tell you what I've got planned. You'll have time to freshen up and then I thought we'd drop by the funeral parlour before they take Dad to the church for the Rosary at 7 o'clock. Tomorrow, the funeral's at 2.00. I think I told you the wake's going to be at Molly Gleave's house. The next day we're going out to the farm.

Donna and Erueti thought you might like that. They've got horses, if we want.'

'Horses? You're kidding!'

'On Monday we drive down to Wellington. We eat at the Kiwiana and you'll see my new house at Eastbourne. You should look through some family stuff. Photos. Silverware. Anything you want to take back with you. Tuesday morning we take off in the car for a slow three-day drive to Auckland. I'll show you the itinerary, a night at the hot springs at Taupo, a trip to Coromandel. There'll be time to look around Auckland and all your old haunts from your Art School days. If there's anything else you want to see.'

'Bea –'

'When you want time on your own, you can feel free to wander off. Relaxation, that's the main. Where's that waiter with the bill?'

'Bea, I'm flying back to the States Tuesday.'

There is a stillness at the table. Do I imagine that everyone in the restaurant has stopped talking? Yes I do, but I am not exaggerating the quality of Bea's stare. She says, 'Tuesday?'

'Yes.'

'This coming Tuesday?'

'I'm sorry. I know I said a week but some really important things have come up and I had to change – Bea?' I push my chair back. 'It's almost a week if I include travelling time.'

She brushes some crumbs from the tablecloth and for a while doesn't say anything. Then she shrugs. 'Well, that's the way it is, I suppose. Francis, dear, see if you can find that waiter.'

I come out of the shower, one towel around me, another twisted over my hair, and see that she has left my suitcase in

56

the doorway. She is still upset. I pick up the case and look at her filling an electric kettle at the sink. The strong side light flattens the colour of her dress and hair and simplifies her to a Toulouse Lautrec poster. I put the suitcase on my bed, unlock it and call, 'Bea, I just worked out what's missing?'

'Missing?' She is at the door, carrying the electric kettle.

'Two and a half hours together and not one word about your love life.'

'Oh.' She lifts the lid of the kettle, looks inside, puts it back. 'I didn't know I was that bad.'

'I'm not saying bad. I'm saying unusual.'

'Well, I have to be careful with Frank and Chloe.' She comes in, trailing the cord and plug, and stands beside the bed. 'That boy is so. I don't know where he gets it from. Judgemental. Not from Barry or me. Did I tell you I heard Barry's got diabetes? That's a shame. Poor old Sol's in bad shape too, had a triple bypass in June. I sometimes think Frank and Chloe can't forgive God for the way babies are made. I just don't dare mention. Not that there's anyone to mention, not for months now.'

'What about the chef? The guy who put liqueur in your navel. What's his name again?'

'Rawson.' She laughs. 'Oh, Diddy! That's ancient history. No, there's just no one and it's such a nuisance. No one ever told me I'd think as much about love in middle age as I did when I was young. Why don't they tell you that? What I want is someone nice and steady like your fellow Lal. I thought he might have come with you this time. Does he smoke? Some people won't go on those long smokefree flights. It drives them mad.'

'Bea, he's not my fellow Lal and no, you don't want someone like him. But you have reminded me that I do need to call him. Is that okay? I've got a card.'

'Yes. Yes, of course, I was just going to make a cup of tea, anyway.'

Lal's voice lifts with pleasure when he hears mine and I am overcome with the desire to be back in the apartment. It is now after 10 pm Friday in New York but I'm not leaning down the phone towards a Friday. It is Sunday I want, our Sunday, the one day in the week that's free of everything except ritual. Nine o'clock he gets up and goes out, unshaven, for the paper. I make the coffee. We sit by the windows, he in the leather chair, I spread out on the couch with one of his mother's cushions, red chain-stitch and little mirrors, at my back, to drink coffee and divide up the *Sunday Times* like so much fresh bread between us. In summer we sit without clothes, although Lal sometimes wears a pair of old brocade scuffs, and the sun, filtered of smog by the stained glass, falls across our skin in long scarfs of jewelled colour. About 11.30 am we dress and go down to 2nd Avenue for a long brunch with a glass of wine. Afternoons we walk and then take in a matinee performance, theatre perhaps, or something at the Lincoln Centre or maybe it's a Guggenheim exhibition or a showing at the Metropolitan. Sunday night we eat ice-cream. We know every flavour of every brand and when we find a new one, our triumph is tantamount to winning the Kentucky Grand Derby. One ritualistic scoop of ice-cream in a plain glass dish. Sacred time.

Lal tells me that all is well at the office and I remind him that he would not recognise a catastrophe if it bit him on the butt. He assures me he would. He says they have the Brewster's Tiffany lighting and the marble tiles exactly the right colour and if I check my e-mail, he and Aaron have sent a video clip with a complete update on both. Then he says would I mind if his mother uses my room for a visit and will I please give his regards to my sister Beatrice and her family.

When Beatrice taps on my door I am in my robe, setting up my computer and looking for a power outlet. She is carrying a cup of tea. 'Everything all right in New York?' she asks. 'I thought you'd like a cuppa before we go to the funeral parlour. They'll be screwing down the lid about five o'clock.'

'Thanks, Bea, but I'll give it a miss. The funeral parlour. My last sighting of him wasn't wonderful, but he was alive and he was our Dad.'

'They're expecting us,' she says, setting the tea down next to the computer. 'I made an appointment.'

'You go.'

'I've already been. With Frank and Chloe. There's nothing to worry about, Diddy. He looks lovely, really lovely, and his grey suit.' She looks at the computer. 'Are you going to do some work?'

'No. I'm going to sleep. But first, I'm checking my e-mail. Lal, by the way, said to give you his regards.'

'That's nice. Oh well, suppose I'd better ring the undertaker. Funeral director. Why did they change that? Undertaker was a perfectly good word. Although, when you think about it, it's funny. Under. Taker. What does it mean, exactly?'

'Hang on Bea,' I sit down in front of the computer. 'You might like see this video clip of Lal and Aaron in the office. Wait a minute! My office! Oh my God, look at the mess, will you? Bea, believe it or not, that's my personal office. Underneath those light fittings and marble tiles there is a desk and the phone I talk to you on. Look at those two. You know what they're doing? Sending me up. That'll be Aaron's idea. He was born making jokes.' I don't have sound but the picture is eloquent, Lal and Aaron straight-faced, playing poker with squares of marble, every bit of my floor and my desk covered with stuff. 'They know I have this thing about clutter. It makes me crazy. Lal will be standing by the phone, waiting for my scream.'

'He looks nice,' said Bea. 'You didn't tell me he was Jewish.'

I close down the computer. 'He isn't.'

'Why is he wearing one of those, you know?'

'Yarmulka? That's Aaron.' I pick up the tea and sip it. It's cold.

'The other one is Lal,' she says.

'That's right.'

She is still for a moment, then she walks out of the room. She is so quiet I know that she is standing somewhere near the door, not moving. I get out of the chair. 'He and I are both new citizens. He was born in Singapore. His mother is Tamil.' Then I wonder why I feel I have to tell her this. I go to the door and see her like a statue on the other side. 'I thought you'd like to see my office.'

'You didn't know we were going to see your office,' she says.

I recover. 'I meant the larger office. Bea, I know a computer screen is an odd way for you to meet him but you were just saying –'

'I'm fifty-five,' she says. 'You are fifty-eight. Why do I get the feeling that I'm a little kid with a big sister who has always shut me out of her life?' Tears fill the shelves of her lower lids. She blinks and the drops run down her red cheeks.

'Oh Bea.' I put my arm around her. 'It's just the distance. We're so busy, you and I. The years go by and I'm not good at writing. I'm really sorry about the trip to Auckland but we still have lots of time for catching up.'

She wipes her face. 'You need to get some sleep.'

'I think you need a nap too. You were with Dad all that

time. You had the arrangements, the motel, Francis and Chloe, my itinerary.'

'I'm all right.'

Her face has closed and I am lost. It's a stupid thing, I know, but it comes way back from childhood. While she was whining and demanding, I could manage a space between us but every now and then she would haul off and shrivel up into this pathetic little silence that would make me feel just awful.

'Bea, we both need sleep, but first there's something I want to tell you. I couldn't talk about it over the phone.'

'Oh?'

'Can we sit down?' I pull out a chair for her. 'You know these days I'm not a practising Catholic. Not a practising anything. Well, the day Dad died, something happened that kind of bowled me.'

Her face is getting soft again.

'I can't explain it. I don't know how to explain it. Last Tuesday at sixteen minutes past four in the afternoon, I knew that Dad had gone.'

'That was before I phoned you?'

'Three-quarters of an hour before you called me.'

She inhales and holds her breath for some seconds, then she exhales noisily and says, 'I was in the hospital cafeteria having breakfast.'

'There's more, Bea. It wasn't as simple as just knowing. Dad was there. In my office.'

She frowns. 'What do you mean, he was there?'

'Well, this is the bit that's got my head around back to front. I was sitting at my desk reading a price list, fabrics for drapes and loose covers. Suddenly, the entire room was filled with his presence.'

'How do you know it was him?'

'Bea, it was Dad. His energy, his life. It wasn't an apparition but there was something else. Dad's smell. The way he smelled when we were young, his skin, his hair, the smell of his flannel shirts, the sheep smell, smoke from his cigarettes. My office was full of it.'

Bea says, 'It'd be someone outside your door smoking. Or outside your window.'

'Forty-third floor? His stinky old Park Drive tobacco? For a while I tried to rationalise the whole experience. Why a smell from forty years ago? If it was Dad's soul or spirit, wouldn't he be dragging hospital smells? Then I had this crazy thought that maybe he would have brought a smell that I would recognise. Just to say goodbye and let me know he was okay.'

Bea looks at her hands and doesn't say anything.

'I wanted to tell you. I wanted to find out what you thought about it.'

She stands up so quickly that her chair falls over. 'You know what I think? I think you should go to sleep or you'll be snoring off during the Rosary,' and she goes to her room.

I pick up the chair, wondering what I said to offend her. Does she think that a good Catholic soul should not wander across the world on its way to heaven? Has Rome not said anything about that? Or does she think I made it up?

I guess that now is not the time to tell her that I won't be going to the Rosary tonight.

I wake from a deep sleep and a dream that I am fighting my way through a crowd at Grand Central Station. I am hot. Motels over here have no air-conditioning. Bea is knocking on the door and calling, 'Six o'clock, Diddy. You awake? We leave in half an hour.'

I kick off the sheet and lie on top of the bed in the orange glow from the closed curtains, wondering why motel rooms all over the world are so ugly, so predictable. If a decorator were employed, function could be combined with aesthetic quality so that instead of feeling institutionalised, our senses could take a vacation. Originality. Beauty. They're not expensive. This motel boasts 'all the comforts of home' but don't folk want to be away from home? Isn't that precisely the point? Oh Bea, will you stop knocking like a demented woodpecker?

'I'm awake.'

She opens the door. 'It starts in an hour.'

I sit up on one elbow. 'Bea, I'm not going to the Rosary.'

She has one hand on the doorknob, the other one the wall. 'What's wrong?'

'There's nothing wrong. I'm going to the funeral tomorrow but look, I don't do this other stuff. I told you. I'd feel a hypocrite.'

'But it's not about us, Diddy, is it? It doesn't matter what we do or don't do. It's for Dad. You know the devotion he had to the Rosary. He and Mum every. Diddy, you went to Mum's Rosary. I remember.'

'And I felt a hypocrite.' I sit up and pull the sheet around my knees.

Her hand slides down the wall to her side. She leans against the doorway, holding her breath. After a while she says, 'Diddy, this means a lot to me. You being there.'

'I'm sorry, Bea. I really am sorry. I feel I've been dropping one disappointment on you after another. I'd understand if you threw something at me.'

'People are expecting you to be there. I told them. I told Father O'Donnell.'

'Say I'm jet-lagged. That's the truth. Tell them I'm asleep.'

'The truth is you don't want to go. Suppose I tell

everyone that? My sister has flown halfway around the world to pay her respects to her father and now. Why not? I don't know. She fails to put in an appearance because. Well, she's lapsed. So what? What's that got to do with her father?'

'Bea, don't push!'

'It wouldn't hurt. You could do this one thing instead of always thinking of your precious self. You could do it for Dad.'

'No!' I swing my legs over the side of the bed. 'I'm not going!'

'How much time did you give? Tell me! A visit on your way to somewhere else. Postcards. Mum and Dad's fridge was covered. New York, New York. I was sick of the sight of wonderful New York. Where were the letters, huh? Where was the time?'

'That's not fair, Bea. I used to call them.'

'After Dad had his stroke. What then? One visit in five and a half years. Oh whoop-de-doo!' Out she goes, slamming my door.

I fall back on the bed, my heart hammering, wonka, wonka, like an old piston. I'm much too old for such alter-cations, although I can't confess to surprise. I put my fingers to the pulse in my neck and wonder why it is that in fifty-five years I have not developed some immunity to my sister Beatrice. Or she to me.

A few minutes later she is back, dressed in a flowing suit the colour of rust, her hair clipped back with a comb. She has gone into her quiet phase. 'You are definitely not coming.'

'No.'

'I don't know what I can tell Frank and Chloe.'

'Tell them what you like, Bea. I don't mind.'

'They know you had a nap this afternoon,' she says, still trying.

'Then tell them in all honesty I can't. Tell them that old stuff is no longer my scene.'

'They won't understand, Diddy. This is about Dad. Not your beliefs.'

'Look, will you do me a favour, Bea? Don't call me Diddy. It's Delia.'

She sucks in her breath.

I make a joke of it. 'It's fifty-four years since you had trouble pronouncing my name. For goodness sake, Bea, I'm nearly a senior citizen. Have you thought how silly it is for a grey-haired old lady to be called Diddy?'

'All right, Delia,' she says, turning to go. She puts her head back through the doorway. 'By the way,' she says. 'It's Beatrice.'

5
BEATRICE

'Hail Mary, full of grace, the Lord is with thee. Blessed art thou amongst women and blessed is the fruit of thy womb Jesus.'

I can't stop crying. I can't. Chloe passes tissues to Frank – Francis – and he passes them to me without looking, kneeling stiff-backed, eyes front, think, bloody silly mother goes to her Dad's Rosary without tissues or handkerchiefs but what do you expect? No, no, he wouldn't say bloody.

'Pray for us sinners now and at the hour of our death. Amen.'

It's not the eyes. Why do we always think eyes when someone says tears? It's the stuff that runs down the nose that's so embarrassing.

'Blessed art thou among women and blessed is the fruit of thy womb Jesus. Holy Mary, Mother of God.'

Some of the nurses from the rest home are here. Parishioners they knew. Sister Monica and Father Bill Hanson and Father Daley. Monsignor Loughnan is getting a bit doddery, poor old soul. I remember him sitting out in the back porch. Dad's smoking place. Talking about football and the price of wool. She made up that thing about Dad being in her office. I know she did. When I phoned her she asked me when it happened. She wouldn't have said that if she already. Guilt, probably. Guilt and one-upmanship. Maybe jealousy, I mean, it would be. It was always me who helped Dad on the farm. I was Uncle Jack's favourite. She's a designer, makes up her own reality. Oh, sweet Jesus, I shouldn't be thinking like. It's because all this week. I'm not myself when I'm tired. Threnody. Now why did I think of that? What does threnody mean when its at home? Something to do with grief? They should have a pill for it, some little aspirin. Because it is physiological, this pain that fillets me like a fish. My chest is full. It runs down the inside of my arms and into my fingers. It's in my bowels, my legs. But I know it's not aspirin I need. Not tea and sympathy. There are women friends any number. We dress up, all beads and bunions and sit in a circle, printing our lipstick on bone china cups, all thinking the same. All feeling empty and unused. Not much I can do about it, though.

Frank puts his arm around my shoulder. That's nice. He's a lovely boy and he lives in Sydney. He removes his arm to give me another tissue.

'Blessed art thou among women.'

Should it be among or amongst? You hear a thing a million times and don't remember. In winter we'd kneel in front of the wood stove. I'd get creases in my knees from the. It was coir matting made from coconut fibre, really hard. Little bits of wood chips and ash. They were slow, both of them. One word, another word, ages and ages for just one decade. At school, Sister Patricia used to say the Rosary like lightning. Us girls kneeling in class and her words all running together in that lilting. Irish as paddy's pig, she used to say. Rattling her big black beads like Jaffa lollies. Frank's got amethyst rosary beads. Never saw those before. I bet

Chloe bought them for him. Merry Christmas, Francis, here's the present you've been waiting. Oh shut up, Bea. You're at it again. Bless me, Father, for I have sinned un-charitable thoughts about my sister and about my. She could have told me she was pregnant again without me hearing it from Frank. Frank? Who's Frank? You know any Frank around here apart from the one lying in the coffin? Named him after his grandfather but now it's got to be Francis. Sweet Mary, Joseph and Jesus, you'd think I could stop this bloody crying. I reach across to Frank for more tissues. I'll have to do better than this at the funeral tomorrow. It's all turned out so. She says she's going to the funeral but what if. You never know with her. It's not fair. She just swans in when she feels like it. Oh shit, you'd think you could turn off tears, wouldn't you, as easy as blinking your eyes or closing your mouth?

The flowers look good. Molly's work. I don't know what Diddy will say about sunflowers. Delia now. That's the way it is. Sunflowers on the coffin but she wasn't here, was she, and that's what. Every year he grew them. The undertaker said they were. Not beautiful. Not perfect. Radiant was the word. The sunflowers were radiant. He must have a long list of words for. His job, of course. I forgot that sunflowers close up like cups in the evening. Although it's not yet. Long rays of sun like searchlights through the windows.

He'll be here all night. In the dark with the little red sanctuary light and the smell of flowers. And Joseph with his chipped toes. And Mary. And her son up there. And the pew he sat in. They sat, we, four of us, three when she was playing the organ for the choir. He never knelt or stood up fast enough. Everyone on their feet, Frank Munro still coming up. Like an echo. Big hands never turning over the missal page fast enough. Handkerchief coming out of his pocket.

Unfurling slowly like a white sail. To blow our noses after we'd wiped them on our sleeves. They were married in this church. Well, no. I told Chloe that. But I think it was a church in Hastings. Doesn't matter. We were baptised here. I forgot to say to Diddy. Delia. What about her baptism? What does she think about that? It's the first time he's been in this church for five and a half years. Hospital, nursing home, back to hospital. He'll never come here again. Never. I know she didn't make it up. He'd have done just that. I was by him all night, the whole bloody night. The minute I went into the cafeteria. It's not fair!

But it's not Dad. Not really. Who am I trying to deceive? I've known it forever, the empty tea cup, the filleted fish on the slab of ice, threnody, threnody. Dear God, I don't know why it never lasts. There is always something happens, always a reason. And when love is dead it's as bad as anything dead. That's what I'm feeling. That's it. My own death spreading like frostbite inside. Hail Mary, full of grace. Pray for us sinners now and at the hour.

The truth is I'm not alive if I'm not in love.

She's not in bed. She's sitting on the couch in her dressing gown watching a games show on TV. She gets up to turn it off but she doesn't ask me how it went. She can see. Well, I'm not going to say anything. There's only so much a person can.

'Do you feel like some supper?' she asks.

'No thanks.'

'You must be hungry.'

'No.' I notice she's left a coffee mug on the bench. 'We had tea and sandwiches at the presbytery.'

'Oh, well, that's fine.'

'Yes. I'm going to bed. Good night.'

'You don't want to talk?' she says.

'What about?'

She fidgets with the remote control gadget. Turns it end over end. 'When you called me, I said I was looking forward to talking over a bottle of wine. I haven't got any. Are you really going to bed?'

'I'm tired.'

'I didn't bring any wine, so – is there a liquor store where we can buy some? Or does everything still shut down at sunset?'

'It's not only America that's in the 1990s,' I remind her.

'Well, great. We'll go in your car. You lead the way.'

'In your dressing gown?'

'Sure. I won't be getting out. I wouldn't know what to buy anyway. The wine we had at lunch was really good.'

'All right. If that's what you want.' I pick up the car keys. 'But I do not want a late night.'

'Who does?' She strides to the door, wrapping her dressing gown tight around her. She's thin. Thin as a rake.

'You've lost more weight,' I tell her.

She grins. 'I know someone who found it.' Then she says, 'Oh come on, lighten up, will you?'

That's okay. She can say what she likes. I just go out to the car, unlock it, get in and wait for her to do the same. It's a warm night. The heat of the sun lingers in the darkness and there are stars. It'll be a fine day tomorrow for the funeral.

She says, 'In New York we wouldn't drive at night with the windows down.'

'I didn't know you had a car.'

'Not a car. What do you call them? Vans, I guess. Covered trucks for work.' She wraps her dressing gown around her knees. 'I keep thinking we're going to have a head-on collision. I just can't get accustomed to driving on the wrong side of the road.'

'You should stay a little longer,' I tell her. 'You'd get used to it again.'

I park outside the Esplanade Tavern bottle store. She gives me a handful of money. I accept it. She says she remembers I always liked cabernet merlot and maybe I could find a couple of bottles of good stuff. I buy three bottles of chardonnay and three of sauvignon blanc. There is no change.

All the way back to the motel she tries to make conversation. At one point I nearly tell her it's not that easy to put right, but it would have been too. It would give her an opening. She comments on the motel gardens and asks about the horticulture course I did when I left school. Oh whoop-de-doo! Nineteen fantastic sixty-one!

'I don't remember much.' Shall I tell her? Out in the freezing rain pruning the roses while Dad was hanging her painting in the lounge? Diddy's marvellous painting?

As I park the car, she says, 'Who's the young guy in the motel office?'

'I haven't a clue.'

'I thought you knew him.'

'No.'

She laughs and takes out a bottle. 'It was the way he spoke to you this afternoon. Sorry. I thought you had a little thing going.'

'No.'

She runs for the door, the grey silk dressing gown flying behind her like a flag. She could at least have put some underwear. She can't have forgotten that much. She's so skinny. Thigh bones sticking out like. The key turns and she rushes in with the bottle while I pick up the bag with the other five, climb out of the car and lock the door. I'm hot. My suit is sticking. Static electricity and perspiration.

* * *

One glass, I tell her, and then I'm into the shower and bed. I sit in one of the armchairs and she passes me a straw-coloured chardonnay. Not bad. Chilled but not too cold. 'What do you want to talk about?' I ask. Although ever since we went out she's been talking non-stop. I suppose she's coming to it. Wanting to know about the Rosary.

'Tell me about Dad,' she says.

'What about him?'

'After he went back to hospital. The last days.' She takes her wine to the couch, wraps herself up in her dressing gown and puts a cushion at her back.

'There's nothing to tell.'

She waits, looking at me over the glass. We still have the same-coloured eyes. Eyes change with. Ours have stayed. Mum said it was the only way the world knew we were sisters. Not hers, not Dad's but our grandmother's eyes, pale grey with flecks of yellow.

'It was gradual,' I tell her.

'Did he recognise you?'

I sip, wondering if I should say yes. 'I don't know.'

'He would have known you were there,' she says. 'It would have meant a lot to him.'

'The nurses said he could hear. Maybe he could. It was hard to tell.'

'You talked to him?'

'I talked. I held his hand.'

She nods. 'I am so glad. So glad you were there. Did he have tubes? You know, intravenous whatsacallit? Were they giving him oxygen?'

'No. They don't do that. Just a catheter for his bladder.'

She shudders.

'There was one thing. I had a little radio cassette player by his bed. I played tapes. All night, piano tapes. "The

Appassionata", Chopin Nocturnes, some Brahms, some Mendelssohn. Mum's pieces. Oh yes, that little Mozart sonatina and the "Moonlight Sonata".'

'You did?'

'Yes. They said. He couldn't see but he could hear.'

'You played Mum's repertoire for him?' She leans forward, dripping wine on her dressing gown.

'It wasn't Mum playing. I don't know where her tapes. They weren't good quality anyway. With the fridge humming. The wind outside. These were just some old. Peter Frankl, Gary Grafmann, Daniel Barenboim, some others. I thought if he could hear.'

'I think that's simply wonderful. Not only were you with him, holding his hand, talking to him. He was cocooned in her music. I know, I know. But for him it would have been her music. It would have been Mum playing for him.'

'Maybe. Maybe not.'

She brushes the wine marks on her dressing gown. 'Does this leave stains? Remind me sometime to tell you about my Italian robe. It's great wine. Want a refill?'

'I'm going to bed. Tomorrow's a long day.'

She is already off the couch and holding the bottle by its neck. 'Sure. But we might as well finish the bottle. It'll help us sleep.'

I hold out my glass and she fills it almost to the brim. If I had a wine waiter do that, he'd get a right old flea in the ear. 'Thanks.'

'You were with him,' she says. 'Like a midwife. It kind of got to me that Mum died on her own.'

It's on the tip of my tongue to remind her that Dad died alone, too. 'Mum's was sudden,' I say. 'But at least you were over here.'

She shakes the last drops from the bottle. 'You never

know how events will turn in front of you. I flew in for their golden wedding anniversary, thinking they'd be having this huge party.'

'You didn't think that!'

'Fifty years married? Wouldn't you expect a big celebration? They were a bit thin on relatives and friends but associates? Fifty years' worth? This is your life, Frank and Agnes Munro and all that jazz? Dinner for the four of us! And not even at a restaurant. They wouldn't have had a cake if you hadn't made one.'

'It was a lovely dinner, though.'

'Absolutely,' she says. 'That's the last time we heard her play. I wanted her to do the Appassionata but she couldn't because of her hands. What was that? Carpel tunnel? Cartilage? A bit of arthritis?'

'Just age, I think.' I sip the wine which has the texture of velvet. In the glass, in my mouth. Under my skin. 'Two days later she was dead.'

'I think about it a lot,' she says. 'The doctors said it was instant, but then they do, don't they? She could have been in pain for several minutes. Calling for help. He was in the garage with his machines running. He wouldn't have heard.'

'He was sharpening his shovel and spade on the grinder.' Now I'm spilling the wine, but only on the chair. 'You know what Father O'Donnell believes? He's putting it in his homily. He said on her way out to get the mail. Now listen to this. She went into the garage to tell Dad she loved him.'

'That's not right.'

'I know. Dad thought he caused her heart attack.'

She holds her glass up, looks into it. 'He told us both, didn't he? He was in the garden and the spade was blunt. He didn't take off his gumboots. Just went muddy-duddy into the kitchen to get the garage key, muddy-duddy on her nice clean floor.'

'And she went out to the garage to read the riot act. I remember him saying. She was so mad, she switched off his grinder.'

'Just a few hours before my flight.' She turns her glass by the stem. 'I was paged at Auckland airport. I thought it was a mistake.'

'Well, you're going to hear it tomorrow. Her last words to him were, I love you. Poor old Father O'Donnell. I don't know where he got that. Not Dad.'

'Hell no!' she says. 'He showed us the muddy footprints under the key rack. If she'd collapsed in the garage. Who knows? Maybe he could have done something. I guess she was thinking about the mail. Just as well he followed her down there. She could have been lying by the gate for hours.'

'No, it wasn't like that,' I tell her. 'He went back to the kitchen to clean up and she wasn't in the house. He called and called. He thought she must have gone for the mail.'

'I don't think he went back to the house,' she says.

'Yes. He did.'

'If he'd gone back to the house, he'd have cleaned up the mud. It'd be the first thing he'd have done.'

'Not if she wasn't there. Not if he was worried.'

'You think about it,' she says.

'Look,' I tell her. 'I don't need to think about it. He told me he went back to the house.'

She shakes her head. 'It was nearly six years ago.'

'So whose memory's at fault? Mine or yours?'

She doesn't answer.

'He-went-back-to-the-house!'

She almost smiles as she looks away.

I put down my glass. 'You can be so bloody condescend-ing. You know that? You don't argue from your intellect. You argue from your ego. You've always done it. Putting people down. Pushing people away.'

'Let's not start,' she says.

'We should start.' I do not even raise my voice. 'We should finish it. Just for once, let's look at the facts.'

'I have never put you down,' she says.

'Ha bloody ha!'

She waves a hand at me. 'You cannot make me respons-ible for your poor self-image. Yes, you heard correctly. Poor self-image. I admit that when we were kids, I did try to get away from you. You were a limpit, goddammit. This little clingy limpet that never gave me a minute's peace. Always wanting, always whining. It was like the old man and the sea. I had you on my back forever. Don't you remember that?'

'You were very cruel,' I tell her. 'I don't think you realise how extremely sadistic. You were my big sister. You meant so much to me. I'd give you things and you'd throw them away. You'd rip them up.'

'I would not.'

'What about the snapdragons? Remember? Antirrhinums? You squeeze the flowers. The little mouths open like dragons. A whole bunch of snapdragons with pansies and a paper doily around the outside. I was only seven or eight. I thought they were so beautiful. I put them on your bed.'

'I don't remember.'

'You threw them on the floor. You didn't stamp on them. You jumped. Jump, jump! Like murder. You told me to get out and then you threw those squashed-up flowers after me.'

'I didn't.'

'Oh yes, you did. I was heartbroken. I was only about seven.'

'If I did, I'm sorry. Okay? I'm sorry. I didn't know you'd be holding a grudge for forty-eight flipping years. I don't remember the flowers. I do remember that you would not leave me alone. When I got away to Auckland. Even there. You would call me three or four times a week. Delia, it's your kid sister again. You couldn't do your homework without a flipping phone call.' She is shaking.

I'm shaking too. 'I missed you,' I say.

She wipes her mouth, jerky movements. Scrunches up her knees to her chin. After a while, she says, 'I don't know how we got onto this.'

'Mum's death.'

'That's right.'

'I reckon he went back to the house. You said he didn't.'

'God,' she says. She sips and sips. 'Remember how we used to argue? I did not. Yes, you did. No, I didn't. Yes, you did. After a while it got to be yes, yes, yes, no, no, no, and then we really shortened it. One of us would go around making this long n sound, like a high-pitched hum. The other would keep up an eternal hissing, s for yes. Mum and Dad must have thought we were nuts.'

'I don't think they ever noticed.'

'Maybe not,' she says.

'They didn't talk much to their children. Time for school. Have you brushed your teeth?'

'They didn't talk much, period. At a social gathering they'd sit like a couple of statues in a park.'

I pick up the edge of my blouse and wipe my face. 'You may not realise how lonely it was for me.'

She looks at me and away again, tucks her dressing gown around her feet. I think she's going to say something but she drains her wineglass instead.

'Especially when you had gone,' I tell her.

'The children of lovers are orphans,' she says. 'I think it was much worse after that – that business. They were very careful with each other. Shall we open another bottle?'

'We'll never get through it.'

'Just a drop. It's really a brilliant sauvignon blanc.'

'That's because it's a chardonnay.'

She laughs and picks up the empty bottle to read the label. 'So that's the secret. The best New Zealand sauvignon blanc is a chardonnay. We have another bottle of it in the bag? Where'd I put the whatsit? You know, whirly thing?'

'The corkscrew's in the cork.'

'Righty! Just a little splash before we go to bed. A toast to Mum and Dad. Seriously, I think it was a stroke of genius to play him that music. I wouldn't have thought of it.' She grunts as she levers the cork from the bottle. 'It's warm. We didn't put it in the fridge.'

I hold out my glass. 'Be that as it may, he waited until I was out of the room. I came back from the cafeteria. There was a difference, you know. It wasn't just that his breathing. The feeling in the room. He really had gone. What was left wasn't him. It wasn't Dad.'

'Have you ever thought,' she says, pouring. And it's not a little splash. My glass is full again. 'I have, and the more I think about it, the more I believe. He waited for a reason. The reason was not you. It was her. Maybe she came to get him. Does that sound too wild? We don't know these things, do we? It had to be when you were out of the room. It had to be just him and her in the old Romeo and Juliet thing, flitting off together on the next stage of their journey. Heck, I'm sorry this wine is so warm. It's still good, though. Isn't it goddam brilliant? Well, cheers.' She settles back on the couch, her glass high in her hand.

'If that's right,' I say, 'what happened in New York?

That experience in your office. Were there two of them?'

'Maybe so. Who knows? He could have been going there to meet her. For the six years she's been performing at the Lincoln Centre, the ghost of Avery Fisher Hall.' She raises her glass again. 'She was good. She was very good. She could have done recitals if she hadn't been so goddam shy.'

'She did at home.'

'I mean public.'

'What about the organ at church?'

'Hymns.' She conducts with her glass and sings, 'Faith of our fathers –' Then she turns to me and says, 'I'm proud of you for playing those tapes. The passage of music, "Orpheus and the Underworld". It was brilliant. It was profound.'

'Underworld.' I think about that. 'Underworld and undertaker. Do you suppose there is a connection between those two words?'

'What?'

'Undertaker. Underworld. Are they from the same? Word, word. Family. Language. Same source?'

'Oh goodness, Bea. How would I know? Look, I'm sorry about not going tonight.'

'Forget it.'

'No, I need to explain. We're different. You say blue. I say green. You say apples. I say peaches. I respect your beliefs, Bea. I admire you for them. I most fervently admire the way you've kept your faith. But I'm green. I'm flipping peaches, aren't I?'

'Just forget it, Diddy.'

'No, no. I need to apologise but no one should be sorry for being honest. So you see? That's the paradox. *Vive la différence.*'

The wine is warm and fragrant. I don't know why we ever chill it. Smells like fresh grass. Like a plate of strawberries left out in the rain. Like a man's shoulders. Lovely.

'So I'm sorry,' she says. 'Because I have no faith.'

'Belief is not faith,' I tell her. 'Faith is not belief.'

She nods. 'Peaches are not apples.'

'Everybody changes, Diddy. I change. You change. The words don't matter so much. It's where they take. It's mystery, you know.'

'Oh Bea,' she says. 'I do believe in something. I do, I do. Not any religion, though. Not Catholic or Buddhist or Humpty Dumpty. I just – do.'

'We probably feel the same. Different words, Diddy. A matter of semantics. Two apples. One, two. But one apple is called a peach. Not really a peach. A little red apple. You know, when you start putting different words. It messes things up.'

'Yes, it really does. Music is where I'm at, Bea. Music is it. Music and –'

'Apples,' I say.

'Apples,' she agrees. 'No words.'

'No. Definitely no words.' Then it comes up like a bubble, a burp. Laughter. 'Diddy! Singing with Sister Helena. Remember the choir? Open your mouths, girls. I can't hear the words.'

Diddy throws her head back. 'Oh God! Yes! Yes! I loved Sister Helena. I loved that choir. Enunciate, girls! Enunciate! The festival at the town hall. Feast of the Enunciation. Oh yes! She had to teach us, some different. Not hymns –'

'Secular songs.' I choke on my wine.

'Secular but safe. Not too worldly. Remember that girl –'

'Barbara Vaughan.'

'You have a brilliant memory, Bea! Barbara Vaughan. We sang "My Grandfather's Clock". Articulate, girls. Articulate. And she, Barbara, oh God, she had us leave out. We sang cock. Oh, Bea, I forgot about that. I clean forgot. The town hall was full of people.'

I catch my breath, and start singing, 'My grandfather's cock was too tall for the shelf, so it stood ninety years on the floor.'

Diddy waves her glass. 'It was taller by half than the old man himself, though it weighed not a pennyweight more. It was bought on the morn of the day that he was born and was always his pleasure and pride. But it stopped, short, never to go again, when the old man died.'

We stand up, falling into each other. My wine glass goes, I don't know where. We link arms and dance around the room, colliding with the table, laughing. Diddy stamps her bare feet and turns her head like someone doing the tango. The town hall. In front of the parents, in front of everybody. Dear Sister Helena. Enunciate, girls, enunciate!

'Ninety years without stumbling. Tick-tock. Tick-tock. His life seconds numbering. Tick-tock. Tick-tock. But it stopped, short, never to go again, when the old man died.'

6
1953

Uncle Jack said he called her Buzzy Bea because she was his little honey but he didn't take her up in his aeroplane. Beatrice thought Uncle Jack was so clever that he could be the big boss of them all and tell Mum he was taking his little honey for a ride because Diddy had been and that was only fair, so there. It didn't happen. She asked and asked but Uncle Jack just laughed and said, 'When the lady tells you yes.'

Beatrice remembered her longing to be in the beautiful yellow aeroplane which had danced in the sky for her sister, but she couldn't recall many of her feelings of that summer. There was Uncle Jack, of course. Her heart still leapt like a trout when she thought of him. There was Mr and Mrs Rawiri and the new baby who would one day own the farm. She recalled the softness inside her which corresponded with the softness of baby Erueti in his pram but that became confused with her later memories of Erueti when they swam together naked in the river. Her feelings for her sister were a permanent fixture and not particularly related to that summer. It was like a chronic illness, the ache in her legs and chest as she strove to keep up with Diddy. But for the rest of it, she didn't know how she had felt. Her recollection of people and events was precise and vivid but she saw the nine-year-old Beatrice only in other people's reactions to her. It was as though she had been a movie camera rather than a child with self-awareness.

She spent many hours in the woolshed, partly because of the Rawiris and their baby but mostly because Uncle Jack was helping with the shearing and always there was the hope that he would put on his flying jacket, scoop her up with a 'How about it, Buzzy Bea?' and take her off in the plane without Mum finding out. He never did. He wore a white singlet stained grey and yellow and both he and Dad had thin cigarettes stuck on their lower lips as they wrestled the big sheep out of the pens. Mr Rawiri didn't smoke. He wore shirts with the sleeves cut out and khaki army pants. The men's arms bulged and rippled as they turned the sheep over on their backs and ran the cutters through the wool, each man's arms different. Uncle Jack's were freckled with ginger hairs and knobbly bones on the elbows and wrists. Dad's arms were covered with black hairs, fluffy as a cat, and he had big hands that wanted to stay open. When he closed them on the cutters, they looked uncomfortable as though the fingers wanted to spring apart. Mr Rawiri had brown smooth arms, knotted with muscle and up near his left shoulder there was a blue tattoo of a dragon cut half away by a deep scar. Once Bea had asked about the scar and Mr Rawiri had said it was shrapnel in the Maori Battalion. Beatrice had thought that Maori Battalion was the name of the dragon.

She watched the way the shears slid all the way down the back of the sheep from the neck to the tail, releasing a flow of wool that fell, creamy white side up, onto the floor. Sweat dripped from the men's heads, from the wet hairs under their arms and fell on the sheep. Beatrice could have caught the drops. She could have poked her finger in their arms in the hollows below the bulges and felt the softness next to the hardness. She could have helped them to shear the sheep but they kept telling her to stand back. She noticed that Dad and Uncle Jack hardly ever lit their cigarettes. The air was full of dust and noise and it was impossible to separate the smell of men and the smell of sheep.

Mrs Rawiri was Italian. Mr Rawiri had met her during the war and brought her back to New Zealand to a poultry farm six miles down the road. She had a big bottom like a cushion and big titties to feed the baby. She talked funny as though she was half singing. Bea asked her questions to hear her talk but Mrs Rawiri didn't always understand. It was her job to throw the sheep's wool onto a table, fold it, roll it up and put it in the sack that hung in the wool press. Bits dropped on the floor. Mrs Rawiri gave Beatrice a broom to sweep all the bits into a heap in the corner. Sweeping was the most important job. If it wasn't done, the men could slip in the greasy wool and fall down and there could be an accident.

When she wasn't sweeping wool bits, Beatrice was out in the smoko room, by Baby Erueti's pram, pulling aside the muslin cover that kept out dust and flies, leaning over, putting her finger inside the little hand. Mostly he was asleep but sometimes he would wake up and look at her with eyes that shone like coal and then his mouth would open and stretch and he would laugh, waving the hand still hooked on her finger. The rest of the smoko room was boring, the old electric jug and teapot, stained cups, milk bottle sitting in a saucepan of water to keep it cool, spare blades and belts for the shearing machines, a packet of tobacco and some ciga- rette papers, a tin of biscuits, some sheep drench, dead flies in a dirty window ringed with cobwebs.

They would always come over to the house for lunch,

Dad, Uncle Jack, Mr Rawiri pushing the pram and Mrs Rawiri walking behind them. While they scrubbed up in the washhouse, Mum would put cold ginger beer and lemonade on the table, bacon and egg pie, salad, plates of pikelets with jam and cream, little cakes in paper cases with pink icing and a cherry on top. Lunches at shearing time were special and the table was always pretty with a cloth and flowers on it but Mum never sat down with them.

Uncle Jack tried to be friendly. One day he brought her some paper music but she just left it lying on top of the piano. It was Diddy who tried to play it, only she couldn't because it was too hard. Lunchtimes, Mum walked around the table seeing that everyone had enough to eat and when the meal was over and the men were outside in the smoking place, she sat in the lounge with Mrs Rawiri while the baby was being fed. Then the men would stir. Uncle Jack would stretch his arms above his head and say, 'This isn't doing much for the economy,' and they'd all go back to the woolshed, Mr Rawiri pushing the pram.

It seemed that it never rained that summer and the light was fierce, hard on the eyes. In the middle of the day, the birds were quiet, the sheep disappeared into black shadows under trees and the only movement came from tiny blue butterflies in the brown grasses. The windsock hung limp on its post and near it, the beautiful yellow Tiger Moth sat in its own shadow, blocks of wood in front of its wheels and ropes tying it to the fence in case a wind came up. Only once during shearing season was it windy and then not too bad, a nor'wester that blew leaves about and had the windsock doing a one-legged dance. When iron on the woolshed began to rattle, the men went out to put more ropes on the plane and that night, with the windsock still dancing, Uncle Jack said he wouldn't be able to fly back to Palmerston North.

He'd have to sleep in the woolshed. Could he borrow Frank's sleeping bag?

Dad said, no, no, he wouldn't hear of it. Jack could have one of the girls' rooms. The girls could sleep together.

Both Diddy and Beatrice started yelling, 'My room! My room! Uncle Jack?' but he said he wouldn't put anyone out. The woolshed was good enough. He'd slept in worse places in the Australian bush.

Mum said, 'You wouldn't be putting anyone out.' But the way she spoke it sounded the opposite.

'Have my bed, Uncle Jack,' pleaded Beatrice. 'It's really comfortable.'

'No it isn't,' said Diddy. 'She eats toast in her bed.'

'I do not! Diddy picks her nose and wipes it on the pillow. I saw her!'

'That's a lie,' screamed Diddy. 'Mum she's telling lies again.'

'You can't sleep in the woolshed,' Dad said to Uncle Jack.

'All right,' said Uncle Jack. 'I'll sleep on the couch by the piano.'

Beatrice remembered how she and Diddy had clamoured, pulling at Uncle Jack's arms and yelling. She also remembered how her mother went all funny at the mention of the piano.

'It's not comfortable enough,' Dad said.

'Couch or woolshed,' said Uncle Jack.

Later that evening, Mum made up a bed on the couch with sheets, two blankets and two pillows. She also put over the grand piano a big double bed blanket that reached nearly to the floor.

Shearing was over, transport trucks had driven in to pick up the wool bales and wether lambs, and it was almost time to air out the caravan, pack the food, surfboards, swimsuits, games, leave the cat and dog to a once-daily visit from Mrs Rawiri, and drive to the beach. That summer they were going south, through the Manawatu Gorge, to Foxton. Beatrice had already put out the clothes she would wear and her third best doll Marigold. It was hard choosing a doll. Alice wasn't cuddly, Poppy had a funny smell and she didn't want to get sand in the hair and eyes of her best sleeping dolls, Verbena and Teresa. She also packed the roller-skates she's got for Christmas. She couldn't skate yet but Diddy could teach her.

Then, two mornings before the holiday, Dad said he had invited Uncle Jack. He said it at the breakfast table, as though it was nothing, and Beatrice sat dead still for a moment, wondering if she had heard right. Diddy was silent, too. Then she and Beatrice bounced up and down laughing and shouting and rattling their spoons on their plates. Uncle Jack's coming! Super duper Gary Cooper! Hubba hubba ding ding!

Mum said to Dad, 'You invited Jack Holland on our holiday?'

Dad turned his hands over palm upwards. 'He was shearing every day and he wouldn't accept a penny. Not even a few beers.'

'You invited him without asking me?' she said.

'Actually, I thought he would refuse,' said Dad. 'I did think that.'

'What made you think it?' she asked.

'His job at the aero club. I thought he'd be tied up.'

'He told you he started the job in February. I heard him say that, Frank.'

Dad wiped his hair with his hand. 'Well, it's done now. He'll be bringing his tent and sleeping bag. He said he'd pay his own way.'

'Is he going to sit in the car with us?' said Beatrice, thinking how he could be in the middle with her and Diddy on each side. That would be fair.

'We can put in the other surfboard!' shouted Diddy. 'Does Uncle Jack play beach cricket?'

'Wait!' said Mum. 'We're not going.' She looked at Beatrice and Diddy. 'We are not going on a holiday with Jack Holland. If your Dad wants his company, that's quite all right, they can go on their own.'

'Agnes –' said Dad, reaching across the table.

She pulled her hands away and put them in her lap. 'You and Jack can take the caravan to Foxton Beach. The girls and I will go and stay with Em.'

'I don't want to stay with Aunty Em!' Beatrice began to cry.

Dad said, 'I know I should have mentioned it. But it just slipped out. He said, "What day are you leaving?" And I said, "If you're not doing anything –"'

'You had no right,' said Mum.

Through her tears, Beatrice looked at her mother's face white with anger, the mouth like a knife blade. It was all Beatrice's fault. Dozens of times she'd said to Uncle Jack why don't you come on holiday with us? Why don't you? Her crying got louder and louder until Dad told her to stop it or leave the table.

'The girls and I are not going and that's an end to it,' said Mum. 'I will not discuss it further.'

Diddy didn't cry. Afterwards she told Beatrice not to worry, that they would all go on holiday, Uncle Jack included. Diddy said had Bea noticed that when Dad really wanted something, really, really wanted it, he got his own way? Mum would give in. She'd have to. They could look in the garage for the extra surfboard.

One day, maybe at that time or maybe earlier, Beatrice had asked Mum why she hated Uncle Jack.

Mum had looked surprised. 'Bea, that's an awful word. We don't hate anyone. Hatred is a sin against God and it hurts Jesus.'

Beatrice stood there, waiting, her hands behind her back.

'Jack has been your father's friend for years, before you and Diddy were born, before I knew your father. He's – he's a man's man.'

'What's a man's man?'

'Well.' Mum pushed Beatrice's hair away from her face, tucking it behind her ears. 'Men and women are different. Some men are a bit. A bit rough. They're just like that.'

'You mean like swearing?'

'He shouldn't talk like that in front of you girls.'

'I don't mind.'

'He's what we call a rough diamond. Bea, I told you, I don't want you and Diddy pestering Jack Holland. Girls should have the company of other girls and women. Just you leave him alone.'

But when Beatrice told Diddy, Diddy said, ha ha ha, pig's feathers. Mum didn't like Uncle Jack because he wasn't a Catholic, it was as simple as that.

Both the car and the caravan were pre-war, the car a 1939 Chevrolet and the caravan oval-shaped, made of plywood painted pink with small windows and a fly-screen door. Inside there was a table that could be put down to make a double bed and two seats where the girls slept. There was also a wardrobe, small stove, a sink and bench and some cupboards with sliding doors. Large objects like the wooden surfboards, the tin buckets and the sack with the flounder net were strapped to a metal rack at the back of the caravan. That year there was also the deckchair and beach umbrella that Dad had made for Mum. They had matching blue and white striped canvas and they still smelled of varnish.

Beatrice and Diddy had on their new shorts and blouses. Mum never wore shorts or slacks. She had a green sunfrock with a jacket and a green cloth sunhat that tied under the chin. There was cardboard in the brim of the sunhat. Beatrice had watched it going around and around on the sewing machine. Mum said that if she got caught in a thunderstorm she would be wearing a lettuce leaf. Beatrice wondered why anyone would want to wear a lettuce leaf, then she realised that Mum had been talking about the hat.

They had to travel very slowly, pulling over to let cars pass. Dad said the caravan would shimmy at any speed over forty. Shimmy. That was a lovely word. Beatrice thought it meant shine. She thought the pink paint might glisten with rainbow colours like oil on water and she kept glancing back just in case it happened. Diddy had out her drawing book and was sketching pictures of horses. Beatrice laid Marigold across her knee, took off all her baby clothes, pretend washed her with a handkerchief and put the clothes back on. The bonnet and jacket had belonged to Beatrice when she was a small baby. The wool had turned yellow, it was so long ago.

When they came near Palmerston North, Dad stopped the car to look at a street map. Mum stared out of the window but she didn't say anything. They drove down a street by the river and found Uncle Jack's house true enough, although the garage wasn't nearly big enough for his aeroplane. Dad said Uncle Jack kept his Triumph in there.

'Has he got two planes?' Beatrice asked.

'Triumph motorbike,' said Dad.

Mum stayed in the car. Diddy and Beatrice followed Dad to the house and when Uncle Jack opened the door, they flew at him as they always did. He lifted them up, one hanging on each arm, but when they asked him to do it again he told them to scoot because he needed to throw a few clothes in a bag.

They wandered into the lounge looking at Uncle Jack's things. There wasn't much furniture but the walls were nearly covered with photos and above the fireplace there was a broken propeller that had been made into a clock. They soon realised that in nearly every picture, he was with people they didn't know. This gave Bea a funny feeling, especially when she looked at photos of Uncle Jack with ladies in beautiful dresses or bathing suits.

Diddy said, 'I think these were all taken in Australia. Before he came here.' She was looking at a picture of him standing in front of a plane, with his arm raised.

'What's that he's got?' said Beatrice.

'Nothing,' said Diddy.

'Move over and let me see.' She pushed Diddy and Diddy pushed her back. She called, 'Dad? Dad? Diddy won't let me see.'

'It's a snake,' said Diddy, making a face at her.

It was, too. Uncle Jack was laughing and holding it up by the head. Snakes were supposed to be curvy but this hung as straight as a stick. It must have been dead.

'There are no snakes in New Zealand,' Beatrice told Diddy. 'Only in Australia.'

'I know that.'

Beatrice went around the four walls again, jumping to see the photos hung up high, and when she was sure, she said, 'There aren't any children. No children, Diddy.'

'Of course he hasn't got any children,' said Diddy. 'He isn't married.'

'He's got us,' said Beatrice. She bounced up and down on

the old velvet armchair by the fireplace. 'Uncle Jack's got us.'

'Stop that!' Diddy said.

Dad was in the hall, talking through the bedroom door telling Uncle Jack that he was not to take his motorbike. 'You're coming with us,' he said.

'Oh, bugger it, Frank. You know the way it is.'

'We'll all go in the car,' said Dad.

'What if it doesn't work out?' said Uncle Jack. 'I get stuck with no bloody transport.'

'It'll work out, Jacko. It'll work. My car is your car. Any time you need transport, take it. You don't even need to ask, you just pick up the keys. We're not taking the bike.'

Uncle Jack came out with a small suitcase, a tent sack and a sleeping bag rolled inside a blow-up mattress. Dad helped him to carry it to the door.

Beatrice put out a finger and touched the ginger hairs on Uncle Jack's arm. 'You're going to sit with me and Diddy,' she said.

But when they went out to the car they found that Mum had moved into the back seat. For the rest of the journey all Beatrice saw of Uncle Jack was the back of his head and all she heard from him was talk about Percival Proctor who was not a man but a new aeroplane coming to the Middle Districts Aero Club. But it was all right, because Mum had a pack of cards in her bag and they played Five Hundred in the back seat until they arrived at the Foxton Beach camping ground.

Beatrice couldn't say it to Diddy, so she told her doll Marigold. Under a pine tree at the back of the caravan she whispered in Marigold's ear that Uncle Jack was the nicest man in the world, nicer than Dad, nicer than Father Brennan, nicer than the Pope. She was going to say nicer than God but God was in heaven, not the world. Even though Mum was mean to him, Uncle Jack was friendly to Mum. Not that she ever said mean things. She didn't. She wouldn't talk to him at all or even look at him. But he would keep on smiling at her the way he smiled at Beatrice and Diddy and he would never forget to say nice things.

'That's a pretty dress, lamb chop. Doesn't she look grouse, Frank? Wouldn't think she's had two kids.'

'Bloody good food, Aggie. No fridge, half a stove. You're a bloody marvel.'

'How's my Betty Grable this morning? Still as beautiful as ever?'

She wouldn't look at him and yet it never made him mad. Sometimes he'd stand with his head on one side, smiling at her, and then he'd walk off whistling to his tent which was at the end of the pine trees, near the sand dunes.

The quickest way to the beach was through the sand dunes. If they had a lot of gear to carry Dad took the car and they drove around the road way, but when they were just going for a swim, they would run past the other caravans to Uncle Jack's tent. If he wasn't already with them, they'd yell, 'Swimmo! Swimmo, Uncle Jack!' and he'd come stumbling out in his swim shorts and they would all race over the sand dunes to the beach and the long foaming waves.

Mum never went in the sea. She didn't even own a bathing costume. If the car wasn't there with her deckchair and umbrella on board, she would sit on a driftwood log in the soft sand, minding their towels and sandals and calling out if she thought Bea was going in too deep. Bea was an adult before she realised that her mother didn't swim because she was mortally afraid of water.

Her most potent memory of those first days of holiday was the way her mother ignored Uncle Jack. Everything else was lovely. The caravan was a dear little pink house full of pine-scented shade, the beach sparkled with good weather and Dad was as happy as anyone had seen him, laughing and kissing Mum in the middle of the road, playing beach cricket and pretending he'd swallowed the ball, surfing with Uncle Jack and having swimming races. He and Uncle Jack stood on their heads with their feet against the caravan wall, trying to drink bottles of beer upside down but they laughed too much and nearly choked, the beer spraying out of their mouths and into the sand. Mum did not laugh. She made bread. She washed the tea towels. She rubbed sunburn lotion on Bea's arms and she played noughts and crosses with Beatrice when Diddy went roller-skating with some big girls. But she would not change her mind about Uncle Jack, and every night Beatrice prayed that God would make Uncle Jack a Catholic so Mum would like him.

On the fourth night, a sound woke Beatrice from a deep sleep. She thought at first it was Diddy, but her sister was lying on her back, her arms flung out, her mouth open not quite snoring. Beatrice twisted onto her stomach to look out the screen door and she saw her mother in her nightgown, sitting on the bench by the picnic table, her head resting on her arms. Her shoulders were shaking.

Beatrice kicked off her blanket and felt her way down the caravan to the big bed under the far window. Dad's hand was on the pillow near his face. She shook it. He raised his head off the pillow, turned and put his arm out to the space beside him. Without saying a thing, he climbed out of bed and pushed past Beatrice. The caravan creaked and shook as he went to the door.

Beatrice climbed into her own bed next to Marigold and lay on her stomach with the pillow under her chin so she could see. Dad was sitting on the bench beside Mum, his arm about her, talking in such a soft voice that the words didn't reach the caravan. Mum sat up, her shoulders still shaking, and he put his hand on her hair, stroking it and lifting up the strands, letting them fall again. Suddenly, Mum swung around, hugged his neck and kissed him hard on the mouth. Beatrice watched. They kissed and kissed, not like a Mum and Dad but like people in the films. Then they got up and went for a walk.

A long time later, they came back to the caravan. Beatrice sat up as they went past but Dad turned back and whispered to her to lie down. He tucked the blanket under her chin. 'Go to sleep,' he said. 'Your mother's just missing her piano.'

7
DELIA

'So you had a party last night,' said Francis. He and Chloe are at the door, dark suit, black dress, suitcase beside them. Their smiles are too bright for my head.

'I hope we didn't wake you up,' I mumble.

'We went back to sleep,' Chloe says cheerfully. 'Is Beatrice up? We need to put our luggage in the boot of her car.'

'I think she's in the shower.'

'Car keys,' says Francis.

'Oh sure. I know where they are.' I press my hand to my left eye which is threatening to fall out, and grope on the bench behind the empty wine bottles. Did we drink three entire bottles of chardonnay? We deserve to die.

They go off with the quick energy of the young, Francis carrying the suitcases, Chloe twirling the key ring on her forefinger. They're dressed for a funeral which is appropriate because I feel like one. The face in the mirror tells me that a thousand dollars of laser treatment has gone down the tube in one night of reckless imbibing. I look a hundred years old. Lal, dear slow Lal who measures life with teaspoons, would say, serve you right. I don't think he's been drunk since his student days and that is almost beyond memory, although I do have a hazy image of five of us once sitting in an elevator riding the floors, drinking rum and Coke after an anti-Vietnam rally. Where was that? What year?

Bea takes forever to dry her hair and when at last she emerges, Chloe and Francis have set our table with four places, apple juice, tea and toast. They have managerial skills fine-tuned by a mob of children and simply assume that Bea and I will be eating before the funeral.

Francis says to his mother, 'Are you wearing that?'

She glances down at her rust-coloured suit. 'Yes. I thought.'

'I'm wearing a beige dress,' I announce.

Bea gives me a quick smile and I am surprised at how healthy she looks, although some of that colour might be make-up.

Chloe moves around the table, the pleats in her black dress parting over her pregnancy. 'Funerals are much less formal these days,' she says and I get the feeling that she is excusing an indiscretion on my part.

Bea says to me, 'You're still in your dressing gown.'

'You were in the shower.'

'Well, I'm out now.' Then she looks at Francis. 'We stayed up late last night.'

'I know,' he says. 'I heard through the wall. That's okay. We've checked out and put the luggage in the car.'

'You've checked out?' she says.

'We might have to leave the wake early. The flight's at six. But don't worry. If it's not convenient we'll get a taxi.'

'I'm taking you to the airport,' she says. 'I have to see you off. I told you not to check out of the motel, Frank. I said I was attending to that.'

Chloe says, 'Francis and I thought we should pay our own expenses.'

'It's not what I arranged. It'll be very confusing for the office, I'll have to go and sort it out.'

'No confusion,' says Francis. 'We just checked out and paid for our room.'

'Have some breakfast,' says Chloe.

'I'll be back in two ticks,' Bea tells her.

I have showered, dressed, patched the remnants of my face, swallowed two soluble aspirin and Bea is still not back from the office. Neither Francis nor Chloe mention it and neither do I. We all know what Bea is like when she's zeroing in on a target. Men are like food to her. She can't help herself. A nibble here, a snack there, occasionally a three-course meal. I used to wonder how Francis coped with the continuous change of role models, although the years at a Marist boarding school would have given some stability. He's a nice young man. I suspect that under the veneer of prim efficiency he is quite gentle. Chloe is more difficult to read. It's important to her to be socially correct but beneath that there is a fire which may one day erupt and scorch a lot of people.

Francis says, 'Mother tells me you went to New York in the early nineteen sixties.'

'Mid-sixties. I had a scholarship. From Auckland I went to the Rhode Island School of Design and then to a job in New York. I decorated storefront windows. Not the biggies like Saks or Macys or Bloomingdales. Just a chain of little drug-stores. The pay was good, I was in a student apartment and I lived thirty-six hours a day.' I laugh. The headache is receding and Chloe has made excellent coffee.

'It must have been a very interesting era,' says Francis. 'Everyone talks about the sixties as a time of heightened social awareness. Mother says you marched in the Vietnam War demonstrations.'

I am surprised Bea knew that. Mum must have told her.

'It was a time of rebellion, wasn't it?' says Chloe.

'We rebelled against everything,' I reply. 'We even rebelled against rebellion. Lal, Charlie, me, we shaved our heads to see the musical *Hair*. Lal and Charlie had the words "bald is beautiful" painted on their scalps and I wore a wig of turquoise chicken feathers.'

Chloe's smile gets small and Francis examines his red and navy striped tie for God knows what. I've lost them. Oh Lordy, how do you carry something funny and wonderful out of its time and place to plant it in alien soil? I seek safer ground and start talking about his childhood visit to Disneyland and how he loved the helium balloon I bought him.

While they are washing the breakfast dishes, I check my e-mail and find a message from Momo about a new job on the Lower East Side which I shall need to look at next week. That is all. I call the apartment and find that a company dinner is going on in my absence. Not Sylvie and Aaron. It's Friday night. Antwan and his lady are there, Philippa and Regus, Mark. Mark? I feel a twinge of anxiety. Mark is so talented with the stuff of trees that he should be making violins or warm-bellied Spanish guitars. The veneer screen he did for the apartment on Washington Square is a museum piece. I do not want to lose him but his love for Lal has become so intense that anything could happen.

As always, Lal reads my silence.

'Mother is here,' he says in a tone that contains much more than three words.

I don't need to thank him. That too is understood.

Then he asks me how I liked the video clip.

I laugh. 'You and Aaron! I suppose now you're turning my office into a refuge for the homeless.'

'What a nice idea. So there is a philanthropic bone in

your pecuniary body! We'll have it all set up by the time you get back. How's it going down there?'

'In a few minutes we're leaving for the church. It's okay, Lal. Everything's okay.'

'You sound a little tired, sweetheart. Are you hung over?'

I laugh. 'I'm seriously impressed by anyone who can mind-read long-distance.'

'It's not difficult,' he says. 'Too much wine and your voice is a dead petunia.'

'I know. But that aside, there is no cause for complaint. Please give my love to everyone.'

'Especially to my mother?' he says.

'Especially to your mother.'

We are all reasonably composed by the time we get to the church although Bea is glowing in a way that is far from funereal. When I try to skewer her gaze she turns her eyes away not from embarrassment but to protect herself and the secret of her little flirtation. She is as smug as the proverbial cat with canary fluff on its mouth.

Francis checks all the car doors to ensure that his luggage will not be stolen during the Mass, and we cross the road to the church. As we walk up the steps, a crowd of ghosts rush at us, all the stages of childhood, chattering and clattering at our heels, overtaking us and hushing at the holy water font. I hear the stern swish of the nuns who taught us, see Mum in her stiff skirts and jellybean hat, walking with a white-gloved hand tucked through Dad's arm, and the other families, Daniel Levett with one leg shorter than the other, eyeglasses like the bottom of lemonade bottles, who could sing like all heaven, Marie-Louise the redhead who died of meningitis and my friend Bernadette who became a Mission sister and went to Peru. They are all here, with the suddenness of beggars, so demanding that for a moment I am lost in a crowd and I do not hear Father O'Donnell's greeting. He shakes my hand and asks about my jet-lag. Then he says something about Dad. 'It was a good death,' he says. He has printed leaflets for us. In memory of Francis Joseph Munro, 1916–1998. I see that we are much too early. The church is empty except for the polished wood casket in front of the sanctuary.

Father O'Donnell steps back and looks deliberately at Bea, Francis and Chloe. 'I'll be available if there's anyone wanting the sacrament of reconciliation,' he says. The old fox. He didn't come down in the last shower.

We walk down the aisle to a pew near the casket and Bea says, 'What do you think of the sunflowers?'

The yellow flowers, arranged in the shape of a cross on the casket, have their own ghosts – standing at the kitchen window, on the north wall of the house, in a vase on the table, lying across the lettuce plants after a storm. The spectres gather in the dull space at the back of my eyes and remind me that my father is in the casket not six feet away from my elbow. 'He loved sunflowers,' I say to Bea.

Actually, it was Mum who loved sunflowers which, in retrospect, seems an odd choice for her, and he loved whatever she loved. He grew them for her. He surrounded her with sunflowers and any other kind of sunshine that might warm the cool dark corners of her life. He did not seek to understand her. He simply adored her.

Bea, Francis and Chloe are kneeling in prayer. I look around the interior of the church and am surprised that it has changed so little in fifty-odd years. I remember my First Communion here, Bea's First Communion when she wriggled up onto the seat and asked me how Jesus got from her stomach into her heart. There, by the lectern, is the spot where Father Brennan collapsed and died on Good Friday, which everyone said was a particular sign of grace, although no doubt it was because the poor guy was horribly overworked and Lent was the last straw. The crucifix is the same, so are Mary and Joseph and the statue of the Sacred Heart. All that old kids' stuff. I think it meant something once, although I am not sure what.

Lal and I have long discussions on the objective nature of reality, our ideas running like eager puppies through the underbrush of religions. We hunt down the common ground and play with it, tossing it back and forth, bouncing it against philosophic argument and quantum physics. Lal believes we exist simultaneously in two worlds, a spiritual dimension which is the true reality and this physical dimension which is but a small interlude. He doesn't call it life. The other is life. This is maya, the Platonic shadowland, a small dream. He says that the question of evil and suffering in this existence becomes invalid when we see the space between birth and death as the blinking of an eye. That's the gospel according to Lal.

The church is filling and there is a hum of voices behind us. Donna and Erueti Rawiri come down the aisle to say they are glad to see me. Matthew Sheehan, Aunty Em's son, shakes my hand and tells me in almost the same sentence that he has got kidney stones and a new car. The funeral director, in a very British pin-striped suit with a carnation in the buttonhole, says a few words. No one offers condolences. Dad's death brings a quiet relief.

What gets to me is the music. Bea told me it was to be played before the Mass and I thought, oh my God, not the 'Moonlight' again, but when I hear the notes falling, triplet drops into the hush of the church, a sense of loss fills me to become something sharply physical. I don't cry these days. That's part of the general dehydration that comes with hormone change. And I am far removed from the child who sought displacement hurt by digging her nails into her palms. I simply sit here absorbing the pain which becomes enormous, a crucifixion without resurrection, and I don't know why I have it.

I grew to hate the 'Moonlight Sonata'. He asked for it so often. He would sit on the couch near the piano, his tobacco packet on his knee, and he would roll the next day's supply of cigarettes while she played. He had no aptitude for music. He didn't know one composer from another. He would make comments like, 'That high bit was nice,' or, 'You got through that quickly,' and she would smile at him as though he had said something profound. When she got to Beethoven's Moonlight, though, that was different. He would put the tobacco aside, rest his head on the back of the couch and close his eyes, and his face would get a look that could not be described except to say that his skin shone. It did. It shone as though there was a light behind it.

When I was fourteen I wanted to play it. She said it was too hard, so I taught myself, copying her expression and phrasing. My efforts must have sounded awful but no one said so. Even now my hands are full of it. I can feel the stretch of the octaves in the left, the rocking motion of the right. At the age of fourteen I made the amazing discovery that those fluttering notes were tethered to earth by G, a sonorous G grounding all that moonlight and preventing its escape into the night.

Bea puts her hand over mine. She is offering me a Kleenex. Well, yes, I am crying. So much for the oestrogen fall-off theory.

The church is more than half full, mostly parishioners, I think, and Father O'Donnell, whose prodigious memory has not been blunted by time, welcomes everyone by first name and begins in his dry old voice which still has a bit of an Irish lilt. How old is he? Must be older than Dad.

I am not comfortable here. The church has become suffocatingly small, as has the ritual. Small too, the child who used to kneel here, a matchstick of a girl who once dreamed of becoming a religious sister. I don't know why I wanted that. Even then I could not have lived with a vow of obedience. I think it was the influence of the nuns who taught us. They laughed a lot, real laughter that glinted on glasses and shook veils and double chins. There wasn't a lot of humour at home.

Francis walks solemnly to the lectern and reads from the first letter to St John. He says, 'Dearly beloved, let us love one another.' He looks across the congregation. 'For all love comes from God.'

I am wondering about 51st Street at this moment where it is 10.15 pm. The others have probably left and Lal will be helping Manorama clean up the kitchen. She'll be tying his striped apron over her white sari and showing her affection for him by telling him how lazy he is. She reminds me of the negative drawing exercises we had to do at art school where the composition lay in the space between the objects rather than the objects themselves. When she loves, she scolds and those utterances of endearment now come my way. Oh Delia, you are not eating well. Delia, you should not wear such dull colours. Delia, do something with your hair.

'There is no fear in love but perfect love casts out all fear.'

Lal says that when they came to New York from Singapore, she was a Christian with high heels, western dresses with padded shoulders and shoulder-length hair in a page-boy fashion. Now she belongs to a Ramakrishna ashram in New

Jersey and although she has never been to her parents' India she covets all that is Indian with an exclusive zeal. She wears white saris, sandals, and her long grey hair, knotted at the back of her neck, is without adornment. Devotees of Ramakrishna do not proselytise, she keeps telling us, for they believe that all religions are equally valid. Still, she never stops trying to convert us and she has a few sharp things to say about the Harekrishnas down the road. Manorama may meditate each day and fast each week but she is, thank God, human.

'The holy gospel according to St John.' We all stand and Father O'Donnell grips each side of the lectern with knobbly hands. When I last saw Dad his hands looked like that, white with brown blotches and blue veins, knuckles large, nails ridged and irregular. I look at my own hands, spotted brown and have a sense of us all moving on the same escalator.

'Love one another as I have loved you.'

I agree with Lal that a forgetting is necessary for this existence. If we remembered the reality of our being, we would all be like lemmings, jumping over a cliff to get back to it. But we do carry something from the other side, an awareness of beauty, for example. Where did that come from? It's of little use to basic survival on this planet. We must have dragged it over from somewhere on an invisible umbilical cord.

Lal and I have dissected many a salad or muffin in discussions on the human experience of beauty and we have never come close to defining it. Thank God, there are still large areas of life that escape the tyranny of rational process.

In the 1970s, when it was clear that Lal and I had developed a solid friendship, Manorama's eyes grew bright with the hope for grandchildren. Did she think that the young New Zealand artist had some alchemy that would remake her beloved boy? She did not speak it. We could not speak it. But we both read the brightness, the eagerness, and felt pain for her. She, with the same sensitivity she has passed on to her son, saw her error. The light went out but nonetheless she insisted on treating me like a daughter-in-law.

'Praise be to you, Lord Jesus Christ.'

We sit and Father O'Donnell leans over the lectern, peering at us over the top of his glasses. 'Near to six years ago most of us were at the funeral of Agnes Munro. Frank was sitting right there, as broken a man as you'd ever see. He never recovered from the loss. And I was thinking at the time, that Frank and Agnes Munro were like Siamese twins joined at the heart. Hardly ever did we see a time when they weren't a couple, the two of them in town shopping, at the school, at the Mass, and not just in the same physical proximity, so to speak. They were truly one in spirit, one in love.'

I glance at Bea. She came back from the Rosary last night with eyes as fat as doughnuts but she is not crying now. She is staring past Father O'Donnell, her eyes fixed on some thought between him and the back of the sanctuary.

He talks about the holy love between man and woman as being not only the true symbol of the love of Christ for his Church, the love of God for the human soul, but also a means to it. He quotes a seventeenth century rabbi who said that when a man could not pray he should seek God in the arms of his wife. Then he tells us at length how the love of a couple like Frank and Agnes Munro validates and enobles a vow of celibacy.

'The writer of the St John letter whom we believe to be the beloved disciple himself, tells us that there is no fear in love but perfect love casts out all fear.'

Yes, but why do we hunger so much for the perfect, Father? Tell me where does that come from? Everything in nature is imperfect, in a state of coming or going, so what planted in us the knowledge of perfection and the desperate leaning towards it? Not the experience of the womb. That's not nearly as comfortable as people used to think. Is it like a sense of beauty, another little remembering creeping through the forgetting? And I've got another addendum for your homily, Father. There is fear in love. The picture of Cupid comes framed in fear. The fear of being devoured by love. The fear that love itself will be lost or worse, not returned. It's the fear of being a Mark living with a pain he did not choose but which he holds possessively because it's better than emptiness. And Beatrice. What about Bea and her fear of loneliness, equating that with the need to fill a hole at each end of her body? And me? The jackpot question. I guess mine has always been the fear that I would lose myself in the same helpless, hopeless way that she did. My mother. Oh, they knew fear, Father, especially after that summer. It was a cancerous thing that did not stop with them but invaded the furniture, the walls, the children. I saw her fear at the piano playing Schumann's Traumerei at three times its normal speed, all those dreamlike notes turned into a nightmare of clashing sound and breathless terror, and I watched him in his lonely place on the back porch, his eyes dark through the tobacco smoke.

'There were times,' says Father O'Donnell, 'when you felt that their love for each other filled the whole room.'

And if it did, Father, where did it leave their daughters? Have you thought of that? Have you wondered how two people who are mirrors to each other, find room for their children? I know that when people die it is usual for someone to make myth of their lives, but please, for our sake, don't make great love out of a great obsession.

'Lamb of God, you take away the sins of the world, have

mercy on us. Lamb of God, you take away the sins of the world, have mercy on us. Lamb of God, you take away the sins of the world, grant us your peace.'

Peace, this, peace that. What's so wonderful about peace? Growth is a product of tension, not inertia. Why do religions advocate a static condition when the whole of life is meant to be a birthing struggle? He's done it, now. Dad has. The chicken's hatched, the eggshell remains. But wherever he is I would not wish peace for him. I would not wish a state of no-growth.

Okay Delia, calm down. It's not such a big issue.

Really, I have no heavy argument with Father O'Donnell and the Catholic Church. It's just that living with Lal has developed in me a natural fondness for mental aerobics, especially where belief systems are concerned. Doctrine, as I see it, is partly about control, sheepdogs on paper making sure that the flock stays together and the ewes keep up the increase. But then there is the other part of teaching which is about the remembering of the forgetting. Except that they tend to forget to remember what it's for. Not just Christians. All religions. They start worshipping the words and the entire journey stops with language idolatory. We get stuck, Father, in our own little webs of ideas.

I kneel with Beatrice on foam padding and remember the hard wooden kneelers of my childhood. How did the elderly manage in those days? Did they consider bruised knees to be just penance? Someone is playing a flute. A young man stands at the end of the choir stalls, his fingers fluttering over the silver pipe. Another flute-like sound rises in harmony. It is from Bea's friend Molly who is as wide as a door but who sings a thin silver thread that is utterly pure. *Ave verum corpus*. Her head is back. You can see in her white throat the quivering movement where the sound begins, and then follow the thread out of her mouth to the point where it twines around the flute. *A-a-a-a-a-ve ve-e-rum coooorpus.*

I sit back on the seat. Bea, Francis, Chloe walk past me to go up the aisle for communion.

I have this music at home on CD but Molly is not Kiri Te Kanawa. No, this thin thread, so at ease with the flute, does something else, transforming the notes to the simple call of a bellbird, a sound that sets the heart quivering with thin, pure grief.

Chloe, Francis, Bea come back. Bea sits down and leans towards me. She is holding the little white moon of the host in two hands. She breaks it in half. I open my mouth and she places half on my tongue, then half on hers. She crosses herself.

The wafer dissolves on the back of my tongue and slides away into silence. People walk past the pew, heads down, enclosed within themselves. The music winds itself around them, around the polished wood casket, around me. As I float somewhere between the voice and the flute my body loses definition and I spread with the sound to fill the church as weightless as sunlight. There are no questions, no answers, just a being. And when the music stops, I am still there.

In vino veritas. It cannot be contained in words.

After the Mass we follow the hearse to the cemetery, Bea driving, Francis beside her, Chloe and I in the back. On the open road, a boisterous wind slaps the car and trees shake as though seized with cosmic laughter. The cracking flags at a gas station could be on some Tibetan mountain. The clouds that swirl across a blue bowl of sky form themselves as more flags, more banners, feathers from angels in their summer moult. The weather is giving him a rousing send-off on a road he's travelled for eighty-two years.

Bea says to Francis, 'We carve the half leg of lamb at the table. It's crusted with garlic, rosemary and blue cheese, and we serve it with an anchovy sauce and char-grilled vegetables.'

'You must have pavlova,' says Francis.

'Definitely. We serve it three ways.'

'Three?'

'Francis likes pavlova,' says Chloe, 'but we don't often eat it. We try to encourage the children towards more healthy options.'

'Pavlova is totally non-fat,' says Bea, 'if you put a fat-free mousse on top instead of cream.'

'It's all that sugar,' says Chloe. 'White death.'

'Remember,' I say to Bea, 'the time we came along here in a high wind and we found a sheep truck that had blown over. It was fortunate there weren't any sheep on board.'

'It was right across the road,' she says. 'The driver was standing beside it. He was kicking the roof of the cab and swearing. Boy, was he upset. I hope that doesn't happen to. Can you imagine Dad skating across the road?'

'Mother!' says Francis.

'Something like that did happen,' I tell them. 'It was in the town, in busy traffic. The hearse got to the top of the hill and the back door opened. Out fell the coffin and away it slid down the hill, between cars, past pedestrians. At the bottom of the hill it slid into a chemist shop. The lid opened and a voice said to the chemist, 'Have you got anything to stop this coffin?'

'Oh please,' says Chloe, with an attempted laugh, 'can we change the subject?'

Bea calls back to me, 'What about McTavish?'

'Who's McTavish?'

'You know, the golfer.'

'I don't know any McTavish.'

'You do so. Oh Diddy, you told me.'

'I did not.'

'You did. Oh yes, you did! McTavish was fanatical about golf. He wouldn't let anything get in the way of his game.'

'No!'

'One day the hearse went past the golf course. McTavish now, he stopped his swing and took off his cap. He stood there until the funeral cortège had gone past. You must remember it, Diddy.'

'I've never heard it before.'

'For crying out loud!' says Bea. 'It was your bloody story. McTavish stands there, cap in hand, and the fellow with him is impressed. He says he's pleased McTavish showed that sign of respect, and McTavish says. He says, "Och mon, it were the least I could do. She were a very good wife to me." Now do you remember?'

'I never told you that story, Bea.'

'Yes you did.'

'No, I didn't.'

Bea looks at me in the rear mirror and her eyes are narrowed. She starts hissing, 'Yesssssssssss.'

Francis turns his head quickly. Chloe looks out the windows at the trees in convulsions.

I return. 'No, no, nnnnnnnn.'

Bea and I break down in laughter.

'Do you want me to drive, Mother?' Francis is tense but he speaks in a reasonable voice.

I slide down the seat, laughing, laughing, and Chloe, still looking out the window, folds her hands in her lap.

Bea's shoulders shake over the wheel. Her right hand slaps her left hand several times. 'Shut up, Bea!' she gasps. 'Shut the hell up.'

'You're mad, Mother,' Francis says.

'I didn't, Bea.' My throat is in spasm and the words have to fight their way out. 'I didn't tell you about McTavish. His name was McGregor.'

Away we go again, while the wind bashes the trees at the gates of the cemetery and the hearse gently bounces over the road hump inside the entrance and Chloe and Francis sit still, no thought of any kind showing on their faces.

Doors open. I recognise only two of the pallbearers, Erueti Rawiri and John Samuels. Perhaps Bea knows the others. They carry the casket along a narrow path between the last two rows of headstones, to the covered hole next to Mum's grave. They place it carefully down on the bearers. Francis and Chloe move into the narrow space between it and the next grave while Bea and I stand on the path at the foot of the casket, with a space of grass and trees behind us. As Father O'Donnell opens his book, we hear the wind approaching with the roar of an express train and I turn to see grasses part in a wide path as the gust races through them. I consider the possibility that it's not wind at all but spirits celebrating a freedom dance. Then dust and twigs blow full in my face and I turn back, ducking my head. 'I'll probably be buried there,' says Bea.

'Lord Jesus Christ, by your own three days in the tomb, you hallowed the graves of all who believe in you, and do make the grave a sign of hope that promises resurrection even as it claims our mortal bodies.'

There are only fifteen of us including Father O'Donnell. Plus the funeral director who has handed me the cards from the floral tributes. Where do all the flowers come from? I pass the cards to Bea who slides them into her purse with one hand as she strives to hold down her skirt with the other. Stems of gladioli are battered by the wind. Gerberas and dahlias, yellow roses, carnations, fluttering mauve satin ribbons, a wreath of red poppies and green fern are all blown about like our clothing. For a few seconds, Chloe's half-moon abdomen is outlined in black above the yellow flowers on the casket and I wish that I had my camera to record the moment against that air-washed background. It would have made a fine gift for the future grand-nephew or niece.

'Because God has chosen to call our brother Frank from this life to himself, we commit his body to the earth, for we are dust and unto dust we shall return.'

Although Mum's funeral was only six years ago, I remember very little of it. Shock does that, I guess. It was late autumn and the cemetery was covered with low cloud, granite grey, that released a torrent of rain as we got to the grave site. The funeral director miraculously produced numbers of black umbrellas. I remember that, and the way we held onto Dad who was shaking as though he had a fever.

'The Lord bless and keep him, the Lord makes his face to shine upon him and be gracious to him, the Lord lift up his countenance upon him and give him peace.'

Peace, again.

But the small piece of furniture that is now being lowered into the ground is not my father. He is over the hill somewhere, his thumb and forefinger hooked in his mouth to whistle the dogs around a mob of edgy ewes. He's standing behind the piano stool, rubbing Mum's neck and shoulders with his awkward hands. We are all at the beach and he's holding his panama hat over the top of his Box Brownie, at the same time trying to see us through the viewfinder, myself, Bea, Uncle Jack. Now he's kneeling, one elbow on a kitchen chair, counting rosary beads with nicotine-stained fingers, his slow and separate words filling me up with a screaming because there are only a few minutes to go to the Lifebuoy

Hit Parade on the radio. Those are not times past but still present within me, full of the detail of sight, sounds, smells and feeling. Oh God, yes, the feeling. Childhood emotions never get threadbare with time.

'Go in the peace of Christ. Thanks be to God.'

The funeral director is giving Bea and I each a yellow sunflower. They are bigger than the sunflowers on the casket. Where did he get them? Are these men trained in graveside conjuring tricks, sunflowers and black umbrellas produced like rabbits out of their top hats? He touches my elbow and I realise that he expects me to go forward and throw the sunflower down to the casket. I don't think I can do that. Bea goes first, the wind whipping her skirt around her legs. She releases the sunflower and I hear it hit the wood, then she puts her hand over her mouth as though she is trying to prevent words from tumbling down the hole.

I move up beside her and look at the earth walls of banded clay and stone, the wooden lid which already has crumbs of dirt on it, the cross of sunflowers still looking fresh in spite of the wind and Bea's sunflower lying on its side where his head would be. I throw my flower and it lands with a soft sound on top of the others. Bea tucks her arm through mine and we turn away. That is all. It is over.

We walk slowly back to the car, Francis and Chloe in step behind us. Abruptly, Bea stops. She turns off the concrete path and strides into the long grasses which drag at the hem of her skirt. Then she raises her arms and her skirt flies free like a flag. She stands there, hair wild with the wind, hands stretched out, measuring. 'This is where I'm going to be buried,' she says. Then she lies down in the grass, her hands at her side, her eyes closed. I run as fast as my tight dress will allow and lie down beside her. 'I'll have this place,' I shout above the noise of rushing air. The earth is surprisingly warm at my back, while in front of me, the clouds race away to nowhere on a distant music spun out on the piano by her fingers. Schubert's 'Impromptu in G Flat'. Her hands move like the wind and the wind is everywhere. It bends the trees, combs the grasses, shears our arms and faces.

My nose is filling with scent of pollen which will be hay fever in a few minutes.

Nobody has stopped or said anything. Through a frame of dry grass stalks there is an image of Francis and Chloe walking on, heads down, still wearing the expression of paid mourners. I stand up and reach out a hand to Bea, to help her to her feet. We lean against each other to brush the grass from our clothes and we laugh until we cry.

Molly Gleave's house is only a block away from the church, a small cottage, big enough for a wake. Women from the Catholic Women's League have set out on the table, sandwiches, cake, cups and saucers, while Molly's husband is pouring the other stuff at the end of the kitchen bench. In the absence of good wine, I order a large Scotch and then go to Molly to tell her how much I appreciated her singing.

'Oh! You're the American one!' she cries.

'Bea's sister Delia,' I explain.

'You've got such a lovely accent!' She is a large woman with a bosom like the pillows on a double bed and a face suited to mothering and the pouring of tea.

I look around the room, thinking that human beings are such interesting containers. You never know from the outside what treasure they are. Father O'Connell, now, I wonder if he still carves ducklings and rabbits from poplar wood with a pearl-handled pocket knife? He advances, drink in hand, and I know that if he hasn't changed, I am in for a God commercial.

He says, 'How's the painting and paper-hanging

business, Delia? Going well, is it?'

'Well enough, Father.'

'I'll tell you now a funny thing. Years ago I was in this little presbytery in the South Island. The priest before me had painted the entire bedroom black as the inside of a lump of coal. Now what do you think of that?'

'Well, maybe he –'

'Needed it for sleep, he said. So I went out, I did, and bought the brightest paint in daffodil yellow. Oh, just lovely. But I had a devil of a job painting yellow over black. Why would that be, do you think?'

'You may have needed an undercoat –'

'I like yellow. Those sunflowers now, for Frank. What a lovely idea.'

'That bit of inspiration came from my sister.'

He waves his glass and gives me one of his shrewd looks. 'You'll be in a much bigger parish in New York, I'm thinking.'

'No.' I return the gaze. 'I'm not sure about God and the Church, Father.' There now, I've said it and either he'll give the party line or I'll find out something about the man who likes yellow and carves ducklings.

He smiles. 'All relationships are based on communication, you know. If there's no communication in a partnership, there is no partnership and if there's no communication in the family, the family disintegrates, so it does.'

I wait for the punchline so that I can engage him in a discussion on subjective views of cosmic communication but he says, 'Now that TWA plane crash. What a terrible thing and them not knowing what caused it.'

The wily old fox has sidestepped. Oh well, I guess he has seen it all before.

I join Bea in the lounge and listen to a group of people telling

Frank-and-Agnes stories, the one about the windows being taken out to get the grand piano into the lounge, only in this version the entire wall is removed. They talk about Dad's careful way with money and how he drove thirty-five miles into town to get a pair of gate hinges at sale price. There are more stories of the farming district, of wool sales, dogs and horses.

'We still got that pony Frank sold us for the kids. You know what young Judy used to do? Bring it into the house to watch TV.'

'Old Frank was lucky with that tractor that time. Got thrown off before it tipped. Three times, he said. Rolled three times down the hill then landed right way up and he drove it away, just a broken seat and exhaust.'

From the way Bea nods and laughs, it is obvious that she knows these stories. Most are new to me. It is strange to hear strangers claiming my father in memories that I don't share. The possessive child in me wants to snatch these stories from their mouths and carry them away, tucked under my jacket.

Erueti Rawiri says, 'I remember we were feeding out hay with the tractor and trailer and suddenly Frank said, "Listen!" I listened but I couldn't hear anything. "Listen!" he says again. Well, it was just the tractor ticking over and the sheep running down the fenceline. "Listen!" he said and he turned off the engine. Then I heard it in the distance. The piano. Agnes playing. Beats me how he picked it up so far away with the tractor going like that.'

Somewhere in the story I realise that the group next to Erueti is his family, his wife Donna, their two daughters, their son and a couple of grandchildren. One of the daughters looks exactly like Erueti's Italian mother, a Botticelli angel with large eyes and a faint fringe of hair, fine as feathers, on her upper lip. As for Erueti, the baby who slept in the woolshed only last season in my memory, his curly hair has turned quite grey.

Molly Gleave brings in a plate of sandwiches and, through half-shut eyes, I watch the movement of give and take around the room, hand reaching out, words exchanged, little energies swimming from one to another like goldfish. You could paint it. Some of the impressionists had a fine trick of breaking the hard line of definition by releasing flecks of colour from the object, into the background. Cézanne, Seurat, Dégas, Monet, Renoir, they all did it, and especially Pierre Bonnard. The colours swam over the boundary of outline and tethered objects to space and each other, with bright stitches. Yes, you could paint the people in this room like that, the exchange of energy going out in flecks of colour. I find it interesting, the Celtic view that the soul is not in the body but the body is in the soul. That could explain auras and traditional haloes, the seeing of bright energy spinning out like sunspots. It might also explain why some people like Delia Munro are protective of their personal space. Just you keep your impressionistic splashes on your side of the fence, my dear Bea, and we'll get on fine. I give what I can. Don't ask me to change.

'Excuse me, Aunt Delia,' says Francis. 'We would like to say goodbye.'

As we drive back to the motel, Bea says more than once that Frank and Chloe had no right to order a taxi for the airport when she had been drinking coffee so that she could drive them herself.

'It doesn't matter, Bea.' I am feeling tired and find it difficult to keep my eyes open. It wasn't smart to drink a large Scotch on the residue of a hangover.

'Of course it doesn't matter to you. He's not your son.'

'Bea, let it drop.'

'It would have been Chloe, for sure. She pretends to

defer to him but she rules the roost, you know. Wouldn't let him come on his own. Oh no. Two days and that's it. Dad's barely in the ground and they're in the air again.'

'Bea, I'm sure Chloe came because she thought she was doing the right thing. I'd say she had a strong sense of duty.' I feel Bea stiffen and add quickly, 'If it's any consolation, which it isn't, you're stuck with me for a couple of days. Are you tired? I feel like something the cat dragged in. Do you mind if I have an early night?'

She sits back, opening and closing her hands on the steering wheel. 'It was all right, wasn't it? Nothing went wrong.'

'It was a good send-off.'

'As it turned out, most of the organising was done for me. I was worried though, that no one would turn up.' She looks at me. 'You know something? I thought he might have been there. Jack Holland.'

'That's strange,' I tell her. 'So did I. I looked coming out of the church. Then I realised I probably wouldn't have recognised him. Did he ever get in touch with Dad?'

'No. I don't think so. I heard he went back to Australia.' She moves out in the road to pass a cyclist who is being buffeted by the wild, bright wind. 'He never did take that job with the aero club.'

'I know.'

'And they never talked about him. Not once.'

The cyclist is a young man with tousled hair and a red jacket that is ballooning wide around his body. Beyond him, in the noisy blue sky, I imagine a little yellow plane swept about like a leaf. 'He could be dead,' I tell her. 'I guess we'll never find out what happened to him.'

She sighs. 'Life is so untidy,' she says.

Although it is barely evening, my body clock has totally

wound down. I excuse myself and fall into bed, my senses invaded by the crashing wind and the sun that splinters the window. Even so, it is not long before I am asleep and dreaming of her piano. She has given me some sheet music which I must learn but when I open it, I discover that it's in the form of a comic book. There are two people talking in every frame. In one speech bubble there are the treble notes, in the other, the bass. I am finding this music very difficult. I don't know the time or the key and my mother is saying, 'The timing doesn't matter. It's a dialogue and the key is communication.' Slowly, so slowly, I try to pick out the notes but my hands don't want to interpret this new way of playing. The piano keys are made of newspaper and the music is called the 'Black and White Rag'.

I wake up.

The room is dark. There is a noise by my bed. It is not the wind. It comes through the wall from the unit next door, the one vacated this morning by Francis and Chloe. From the muffled voices, the grunts and the rhythmic creaking, it is obvious that two people are engaged in sexual activity. I roll over, the pillow round my ears, and try to go back to sleep but the noise continues with undiminished energy. Then I hear one voice louder than the other, and I sit up, all sleep gone.

It is almost half after ten and although the light is on in the lounge, the room is empty. Bea's bed has not been turned down, nor is she in the bathroom. I go back to my room, get into bed and face the wall which seems not to be amplifying the creaks and grunts and occasional shrieks. As a voice rises in an oh, oh, oh, oh, I bang on the wallpaper with my fist and yell, 'Quiet!'

There is a sudden and dramatic silence.

As Bea suggested earlier, life can be rather untidy.

8
BEA

The wind has disappeared, not a breath to stir the morning. Funny that. It came up roaring an hour before the funeral and went down right after. Erueti says it's a Maori tradition for the sky to weep for a great man or woman. He doesn't say anything about wind.

She doesn't mention last night and neither do I but I can still feel the glow on my hand where he kissed me when I handed him the keys this morning. Not on the back of the hand like a finger-nibbling Frenchman, but a long kiss in the cup of the palm with his nose at my wrist and his breath bathing my entire hand. That was the first thing I thought. Breath. The day I checked in and saw his perfect ears, small, whorled like the inside of a seashell, I wanted to breathe into them. Silly really. But perfect ears are as rare.

'Do you think they'll be suitable?' Diddy says. She is talking about her footwear.

'You know the farm, Diddy. You know your shoes. Erueti did offer the horses.'

'For crying out loud, Bea, I haven't been on a horse in forty years. I'm too bony. My coccyx would fuse to the animal and we'd become a centaur.'

'He's got a four-wheeled motorbike he'd lend us.'

'After hearing how Dad rolled the tractor on that slope? No thanks. I'll walk.'

We pause at the intersection, indicators flick, flick, flick, and I think of last night and the softness at the back of his neck in contrast to the skin of his chin hardened by shaving. It's always so lovely in a man, this combination of softness and hardness. And the surprise of hair. Sometimes on the shoulderblades or abdomen. Hair thick as a hearth rug. Or a few silk threads. Covering a map where fingers can walk.

'Are you listening, Bea?'

'I'm sorry. I was.'

'Spare me the details,' she says.

It's more than a year since I visited the farm. For Diddy it's been six years. She'll see some major changes, but nothing ever stays the same. That's the way it is. At least she's in a happy mood. The last two days she's been as jittery as an addict doing cold turkey, ping, ping, nerves sounding off like banjo wires. Relaxed now, must have slept well. Knowing her, she won't talk about what happened. Well, if she thinks she spoiled. It was funny. We laughed and laughed and he pulled my head down to rest on his shoulder. Even his arms were soft against me. I like that in a lover, a bit of plumpness. Some women make a fuss of muscle and bone but heck, if I wanted that I'd hug a kitchen chair.

'Tell me the names of the Rawiri children,' she says.

'I told you yesterday.'

'I've forgotten.'

'It doesn't matter because they won't be home. The girls are Riperata and Kiriana. The boy is Ed who is married to Ruth and they have a boy and a girl, Ranui and Tania. Ed is short for Eduardo. He was named after his Italian great-grandfather.

'Eduardo is a Spanish name,' she says.

'It's Italian. It means Edward, just like Erueti means Edward in Maori. His mother told me that when he was a baby. He was named for her father who died in Trieste during the war.'

'Be that as it may,' says Diddy. 'Eduardo is a Spanish name.'

'Well, it's probably both.'

'The languages are similar but not identical,' says Diddy. 'It would be something different in Italian.'

I glance at her. She has got that look in her eye. 'Oh come on, Diddy. You know enough Italian to order a pizza.'

'I do have conversational Spanish,' she says.

'Since when?'

She folds her arms across her seatbelt. 'Eduardo is Spanish.'

'Who cares?' I slap my hands on the wheel. 'Do you realise how ridiculous this conversation is?'

'You're right,' she says. 'You're absolutely right.' She unwraps her arms and rests her elbow on the door, drums her fingers on the dashboard. 'Tell me something. Why did you go into the unit next door?'

'It was empty,' I reply. To our left there is a tractor and trailer in an orchard, a man in a mask spraying apple trees. I'm surprised that he's working on a Sunday. Then I realise he couldn't have done the job in yesterday's wind. 'It had a double bed,' I tell her.

'Two good reasons,' she says. 'Was it worth it?'

'Yes. Yes it was.'

'Three good reasons. All right, what shall we talk about?'

On either side of the road, as far as we can see, there are apple orchards. They are all recent history. When we were young, this was poorly drained land hosting buttercups and rushes and dairy cows that wandered across the road. The cows, not the buttercups, of course. One of the Logans died when his car hit a cow. They said it went through the windscreen but I had trouble with that, a fully grown cow going through. I mean, how could it? The Logans have moved away, and the Pojurskis. The Heinkels' farm is a vineyard. Grapes do well on the river flat. Erueti is thinking of putting the front paddocks into vines. The soil's right, he said, and it lies to the sun. He told me he will label a private bin collection especially for the Kiwiana restaurant and although he was laughing, I expect that will happen. Erueti never makes throwaway statements.

'Tell me about your new house,' says Diddy.

'You'll see it tonight. No. Let's talk about you.'

She seems surprised. 'Me?'

'Yes, you, Diddy. You give information like blood. Like I'm a leech or something.'

'Come on, Bea!'

'It's true. I'm not looking for an argument, just stating fact. You mention names and places but they don't mean anything to me. You seem to think that already I know. Well, I don't. I don't know Lal. I don't know your work or the people. I don't know anything!'

'You would if you flipping came over,' she says.

'You never invited me.'

'What?'

'You never did,' I tell her.

'You're my sister, for God's sake! Of course I don't extend a formal invitation. I expect you to say you're coming and get on a plane. What were you waiting for? Me to mail you a ticket?'

I don't know why she is suddenly shouting and waving her hands. I raise my voice over hers. 'Tell me about your work, for heaven's sake!'

126

We have slowed behind a freight truck which is moving a crate of black-and-white cows with fat dirty rumps. Their smell fills the car, even with the windows closed and I am reminded of running barefooted in long green grass and treading in a cow pat, the crust breaking and the green soup oozing between my toes with a rich, sun-warm smell.

'It's not my work capital M,' she says. 'We have a team of nine and each has an area of expertise. Each is responsible for the subcontractors in that area. Antwan DeLevre runs the painting and papering team. They work hard. You know one person will paint forty doors and door frames in a day? That's right, forty. But Antwan is a funny guy. He'll never hire anyone he doesn't know. By know, I mean he's got this insatiable appetite for inside information, kids' birthdays, age of grandmother, list of surgeries. He buys cards for anniversaries, you know. I think it's a form of possessiveness. We call him Big Daddy. Then there's Aaron and Sylvie Goodman.'

I pull out to pass the cow truck. 'Is that the man in the beanie?'

'Yarmulka. That's Aaron. He's the joker in the team and an artist *extraordinaire*. It's Aaron and Sylvie who have built my reputation. No, I mean it. I still do most of the stencils and gold leaf work but I leave the real art to them.'

'They paint pictures for you?'

'On walls and ceilings. Let me tell you. They'll cover a wall with a pre-Raphaelite rose garden or they'll do a kind of Marc Chagall tree growing up from the floor and branching all over the ceiling with flowers and violins and goblets of wine. They interview the client, then they do the sketches. They work together. They argue. They never stop arguing. But that's just their mouths. The rest is in perfect harmony. They can –' She turns her head. 'Grape vines! What happened to Heinkels' farm?'

'Vineyards all over. There's not much money in sheep, these days. Go on.'

'Aaron's the joker. He tells stories, teases. Always when he does a painting, there is some little joke. It's his signature. In a rose garden there'll be a small bird with three legs. A Paris street scene will have a distant road sign in Hebrew. He's famous for it. The clients always look for the Aaron Goodman trademark. But there was a time when he didn't do it. It was a three-bedroomed apartment on upper Park Ave and the clients wanted to turn one of the bedrooms into a chapel. They wanted a copy of Michelangelo's *Creation of Adam* on the ceiling. I've never seen Aaron so uncomfortable with a painting. He's not fanatical but for one thing, he had a real problem about putting a human image on God. Then there was the appearance of Adam. If he could have passed the job onto someone else, he would have been happy. He did it, though. Sylvie took me in to check the work before the scaffolding came down. It was a great painting, straight off the ceiling of the Sistine Chapel. But, you know, we scanned every inch of it and we couldn't see Aaron's trademark. No joke. He couldn't bring himself to sign the work. I said it was a pity. Sylvie said it sure was a pity with bells on. Then she mixed a palette of paint and skimmed up the ladder. You know what she did? She circumcised Adam.' Diddy winds down her window. 'More grapes. Bea, what's happened to the place?'

I have told her several times that she must expect some changes to the farm but she is still surprised by the vines next door, the new bridge, the carved figures at our old gateway.

'Heads on poles!' she exclaims.

'They're po. Erueti's Maori ancestors.'

'Yeah? But he didn't go in for that stuff.'

We drive slowly between the tall poles with their sightless faces painted the colour of ferric oxide. They are a symbol of a greater change which she has missed. All over the country. Maori identity and Anglo bewilderment.

'That family didn't even speak Maori,' she says.

I change gear and we bump over the drive, ruts hardened by dry weather. 'Erueti speaks Maori, Italian, English, French and a bit of Samoan. He says that Maori is his first language. He and Donna speak it. All the time in the house with the family.'

'That's certainly new,' Diddy says.

Not so new. Diddy has lived away from this country for so long that the slow movements of change must seem as sudden as earthquakes. 'They're going to put the front paddocks in vines,' I say, changing the subject.

The truth is, we tell ourselves lies. Everywhere I go I applaud the Maoritanga movement, the gathering pride of local tribes, the way they claim. Yes, I do. Their land and their language. I do approve in principle. But not my Erueti. I saw him first the day after his birth. I wheeled him in his pram, taught him to say my name. I made him a sailor doll out of a clothes-peg, showed him how to blow bubbles with an acorn and grass-straw pipe, took him to his class on my way to high school. Years later by the river, I didn't seduce him. It wasn't like that. He was fifteen with a deep voice and sleepy eyes filled with loving, and he splashed me. Water in my face, laughing. At his wedding, he said with his arm around Donna that a man never forgets his first love and for the quickest time, he looked at me. That's when I was living with Peter. No. Wait a minute. I think it was Angus. Anyway, I knew Erueti more fully than I had known any other man and then. It was all different. Not that the Erueti I knew changed. It was this other side of him that I didn't know existed. The

Maoriness. Talking to his children and Donna with words I didn't understand. Stopping me when I tried to set the table with an old cotton bedsheet instead of a tablecloth. And this ancestor business, names linked to other families all over the country. I wasn't a part of. He still rode a horse bareback. He still had lovely sleepy eyes. But he was moving more and more into that other world and closing the door between him and me. I hated him for it.

Diddy says, 'Did Dad know Erueti was going into wine?'

'No. He was past knowing anything.'

'Dad and his precious sheep.' She laughs. 'He always thought that synthetic fibres were just a passing fad.'

The garage has been repainted. Where there were once roses, sunflowers and lavender there is now concrete, a shed with three bicycles in it and a basketball hoop outside. Wooden tubs grow green herbs in Dad's old smoking place in the back porch. There is a line of shoes, all sizes and colours, by the screen door.

Donna comes out to welcome us. She wears a faded T-shirt which shouts the words *Don't be happy. Worry!* but the message hasn't got to her face yet and her smile is as wide as the door. As we kick off our shoes, she looks at Diddy's moccasins. 'I think Riparata's got a new pair of trainers about your size. You got time for a cup of tea and some muffins?'

Diddy's eyes are sliding around the walls, touching on the photographs and furniture, the woven tukutuku panel in the hall, the collection of flax baskets, some decorated with bits of wood and paua shell. In the kitchen there is a large poster which seems to be advertising some Maori cultural event but the information is all in Maori so I'm not sure what. Things change. Our table was always by that wall and there's a TV and stereo cabinet where the piano used to be.

Erueti's in the laundry putting a new cold tap over the tub. Here, everything is the same, the washing machine Dad bought Mum with his tax rebate, the yellow and black floor tiles where we used to throw our dirty clothes expecting her to pick them up and somehow magic them into our wardrobe, clean and neatly ironed. Why didn't she make us wash our own clothes? She worked so hard and we took it all for granted. No wonder she needed that piano.

'Do you want me to take you up the hill on the four-wheeler?' Erueti asks. I suspect that the tap has been an excuse to keep him inside until we arrived.

'No, no,' says Diddy. 'We'll hike. We need the exercise.'

'I don't need exercise. Speak for yourself,' I say and she gives me a dirty look. When I said exercise, I didn't mean. What did she think? Last night? Oh heck, you know, you just can't win around Diddy. I think it would be lovely for Erueti to show us around the farm but she's determined that we walk on our own, so that's the way it is, and as soon as we finish our tea, we are off with Diddy wearing Riparata's Nikes and a straw hat and me carrying a bottle of water in a backpack. Donna is a practical woman. She thinks of things like water and sunblock.

I tell Diddy that the Rawiri's old poultry farm is also now a vineyard. As a poultry farm it was never big enough to support two families and in the 1980s Erueti's work for Dad grew from casual labour to farm manager. When old Mr Rawiri died in 1991, his Italian wife, ill with diabetes, moved to Napier. By then Dad had decided he would never get a son-in-law to take over the farm and he suggested that if Erueti and Donna wished to buy the land, he could leave most of the finance in it. After Mum died, the family were always over, looking after Dad. It was a logical step for them to sell the poultry farm when Dad went into the nursing home, and move into the house.

'Do they still do crop-dusting?' Diddy asks.

'Crop what?'

'Oh. You call it aerial topdressing. Do they have that? I notice there's no windsock.'

'That's been gone for years. Just rotted and fell to bits. Topdressing changed, you know. Farmers formed a co-operative to buy bulk fertiliser. There were bigger planes coming in from the fertiliser works. Remember Uncle Jack's Tiger Moth?'

'It wasn't his,' she says. 'It belonged to the aero club.'

'I never did get that ride he promised.'

The grass is as we have always remembered it, summer-dry and populated with small blue butterflies that rise in front of our feet. Diddy wants to know how old grass plants get to be.

'How do I know?'

'You're the horticulturalist.'

'Was,' I tell her. 'Why do you ask?'

'We probably ran barefooted over this same grass. Oh my goodness! The poplar trees! Remember when they were little itty-bitty things with shivering leaves?' She strides ahead of me and throws her arms wide against the trunk of a poplar. 'You know what's tucked inside one of these trees. Your doll's shoe. I hid it in a tiny hollow.'

'Why?'

'Oh God, I don't know. Why did we ever do anything? Oh Bea! The woolshed!' She turns and runs like a greyhound.

I follow, aware that my jeans are ten sizes larger than hers, and we go through the small side door of the woolshed, breathing in the smells of childhood. The lower floor is all gloom and dust, racks of timber, overalls and rusted tools hanging on nails, stacks of paint cans, plastic canisters of sheep drench and dip. I put my hands over my head as we duck under some of the lower beams. There are cobwebs everywhere.

'Look, Bea!' Diddy is lifting up the corner of a large tarpaulin covered with sheep droppings which have fallen from the floor above. It's a heavy canvas cover of a type I haven't seen. Not for years and years. Underneath is the car.

'The old Chevvy!' Her voice is almost a whisper. 'Oh Bea, it's so rusted.'

'Dad had it out under the trees. Erueti towed it in here. He thinks he might be able to restore it.'

I hold the cover up while Diddy wrenches open the door. In the dark it's hard to see detail but the smell of it fills me with the time when cars smelled like cars and not plastic toys. We stand in silence, inhaling the oil, metal, wood, fabric, and riding memories to Foxton Beach. We arrive at that same point where she and I sat in the back seat, staring at the embers of the bonfire and wanting the world to end. She did it deliberately. I can still see the way she got out of the car and walked across the sand to Dad, her hands on her hips. I still remember her words. Does she know the extent of it? What damage she caused?

'Great old car,' she says. 'I hope he gets it back on the road.' She closes the door and we lower the cover, releasing a stream of dry sheep pellets over ourselves.

'Shit!' she says and then laughs, brushing her hair and shoulders.

The upper floor has changed, different shearing machines and a new wool press. The smoko room has another table and by the wall there is a freezer chest full of dog meat. The window still has a lace curtain of cobwebs. It still frames a view of sundry hills and a pole where a windsock once hung.

As we walk up the farm track, I ask her again about Lal. 'Didn't you ever think of getting married?'

She laughs. 'I've told you. It's not that kind of relationship. We have separate lives.'

'You're obviously very close. You live together. You work together. What does he do, exactly?'

'He was a bookbinder,' she says. 'Mostly, he restored old leather volumes. He even did his own Florentine marbling for the endpapers. There was no money in it, of course. Lal is wise in most things but not where a dollar is concerned. Eventually they went broke and he came to work for me.'

'They?'

'His partner Byron moved to Chicago. Lal's been with the firm nine years now. He does almost all of the measuring, the specifications. He's very thorough. Slow, but utterly reliable. He often works with Philippa who's our architect.' She turns to look back at me. 'Who else is there? Regus? He's our flooring expert but he's having a month off on maternity leave. That's why Aaron and Lal were sending me up over the black marble. Then there's Mark. He's like Aaron, another exceptional artist but with wood. He's a big soft guy. He walks like a bear. He did an apprenticeship in reproduction furniture but he doesn't stop there. He can make anything. It's in his hands. Have you noticed that? How people carry their art in their hands? It's as though the hands are directly linked to the soul and the head is somewhere else entirely. That's how she played.'

I shrug. 'I missed out on those particular genes. She said I had no ear.'

'She said the same to me.'

'But Diddy, you played the piano beautifully.'

'Not like her. My hands can pick music from a keyboard. The music was in her hands. She carried it around with her

134

and when she took it to the piano, she made the piano a oneness with her. You know what I said about riding a horse? She was a centaur with that piano.'

There is something like a sadness in her face which makes me say, 'Diddy, you could have been the same. You were brilliant. You just put your time into your art instead.'

She shakes her head. 'I wasn't anything near brilliant at either. Bea, I haven't got what it takes. Originality? The creative fire in the gut? I don't know. I was an executant artist in both music and painting, technical competence but as hollow as an Easter egg. No, no.' She lifts her hand to stop my protest. 'I don't belittle my skills. I'm just pleased that I recognised what they really were, early in my career.'

'I thought you were so gifted,' I tell her. 'You could do wonderful drawing and painting. You played the piano. I really, really envied you.'

'Oh Bea! What a waste of time! I assure you, my appreciation of the arts has always far outweighed my talent.' She laughs, then suddenly is serious. 'I envied her, you know. I wanted so much to be like her. No, not like her. To actually be her. But then that wasn't entirely about music.'

I nod and wait for more. It doesn't come. I think we both feel. Like coming to the edge of the deep river. One more step and you get swept away in the current you knew once and now avoid at all. So you turn away. At all costs.

'There's a good view from here,' I remind her.

We stop on the track while she takes off her cotton jacket and ties it around her waist. Then she changes her regular glasses for the ones with the tinting lenses. Below us we can see the farm out to the road, spread like a stage set. I imagine the actors, four people going back and forth, speeded up like a fast film. She is in her Sacred Heart uniform, running down the drive ahead of me to the school bus and I am

135

screaming at her to wait. I was always yelling that. Diddy, Diddy, wait for me. Dad is on the same drive, walking, hobbling, running. Did he yell too, when he saw her lying near the gate? Yes, there are changes, but our ghosts are still everywhere. It's not the dead that make ghosts. It's the living.

'You know her piano is in my spare bedroom?'

'You haven't sold it?' she says, surprised.

'I haven't sold anything. I couldn't. Not until you.' I start walking again. 'Do you want it?'

'A grand piano?' She laughs. 'I'll need an extra suitcase.'

'Diddy, I'm serious. Do you want the piano?'

'Seriously, no,' she says. 'Even if I did spend the earth to ship it and even if I did destroy half the apartment to get it in, it's old. It's past its use-by date. There's a limit to the cost of sentiment, Bea.'

'I suppose that's true.'

She smiles. I can't see her eyes but her mouth twists up at the corners. 'Sentiment is not a good reason for doing anything. That's why I couldn't go to his Rosary the other night. You were upset. I was spaced out with travel. I failed to make an adequate explanation. It was everything to do with a personal freedom which is very important to me. You know, I have to let go of some things. I suffer from some kind of emotional claustrophobia. I always have.'

'That's all right.'

'I can't stand all that old stuff. It drives me crazy.'

I stop right there on the path. 'Don't knock it, Diddy.'

'Look, I'm not knocking it.'

'I love what you call old stuff. It's me. It's my life. It's.' My voice always betrays me. It swims off in tears, for no good reason, and I turn away from her.

'I'm sorry,' she says. 'I know how you feel. Please, can we talk about this without getting into an argument?'

I nod and she walks a few steps towards to me. For a moment we look down the slope ridged with grass and sheep tracks, then, with a quick movement, she sits down at the edge of the track. She pats the space beside her. I wipe my nose and hear myself sigh. I hate sitting on the ground. It takes so long to get down and even longer to get up again.

'I didn't say thank you for yesterday,' she says. 'There is something. I felt it. I remembered. But God, Diddy, it's so top heavy, buried under a ton of ball and chain. Politics, politics. It's all that old boys' business that I can't stand.'

'The Rosary isn't old boys' business.'

'Yes, it is.'

'How can you say that? Mary is more powerful than the Pope. Just about the entire spiritual experience of the church is feminine.'

'We weren't talking about spiritual experience,' she says. 'We were talking about structure and an old-boys' club which diminishes women.'

'Well, yes, I know, Diddy. But then they have to have that.'

'They don't have to have it. Women have been lobbying for change for twenty-five years and where has it got them?'

I shake my head. 'Take the structure away from the church and what would be left for the men? Women are lucky, Bea. We are. Spiritual things come so naturally. Men have to work really hard to get. You know, it's like scaffolding. Their rational processes. Take it away and their faith falls down.'

'Ha-tiddly-ha,' she says.

'I think women are kind of liquid. We just flow around the structure and it doesn't bother. We fill in the gaps.'

She snorts. 'We fill in the gaps! That's a good description of the role of women. No vote. No authority, not even over their own bodies. For crying out loud, Bea. Having celibates rule on sexual function is like having teetotallers judging brands of whisky.'

'All right, Diddy! We've all heard it. It's an old drum. I mean, it's not the most important.' I lie back on the path and clasp my hands under my head, aware that at any moment she's going to start a tirade about four centuries of witch hunts. 'I have to admit I've always been a bit of a failure. You know, as a feminist. I can't help feeling sorry for the men. They've got so lost somehow in this women's movement.'

'Because their roles are defined by the subservience of females.'

'That's not what I was going to say. I know there have been extremes. Injustices. But they cut both ways. How do we know it's all men? Just because some women say so? I value freedom too, and it's never been men. They've never stopped me. If there's ever been an enemy, it's been another woman.'

She is quiet. I wonder if she thinks I am referring to her. I wasn't. But I can't find a way to say so without her thinking I was. I go on, 'Men are so different. They have this sense of duty and chivalry. They are so protective of women. Suddenly, all that honour has become a crime. It must be like a mother having her baby attack her.'

Diddy is still seated, her back to me, that same stiff posture that Mum used to get. She turns, resting back on one arm, shaking her head. 'Do you realise how strange this sounds to me? None of the men I know conform to this image you have of their gender. You are not describing men, Bea. You're describing the fabricated models put forward by religion for no other reason than patriarchal control.'

'No. No, I'm not. It's not a religious or cultural thing. Men are different. They think differently. And they have this problem. Poor things, they are so fixated on the size and shape of their. You know. They're all convinced they're abnormal.'

'Oh nonsense,' says Diddy.

'They do. If women had to think about their sexual organs as much as men, we'd all have –'

'Tunnel vision?' suggests Diddy.

'I was going to say nervous breakdowns. Seriously, Diddy, I think men have a hard time. And don't laugh. I wasn't trying to be funny. Men do their best to understand women but women make no attempt.' I stop because she is bowing towards me, pretending to play a violin. I feel a small sense of satisfaction. When we were children, she always did this sort of thing when she was losing an argument.

At the top of the hill, we stand against the sky, arms spread to catch a breeze so small and new that it barely ruffles our hair. Diddy looks down to the river and beyond, the mountain range which puckers the horizon. 'I don't remember this,' she says. 'I always thought it was much bigger. The river. The ranges. I guess it's been nearly forty years.'

'Since what?'

'Since I last stood here.' She removes her glasses and squints into the sun. 'When I came home there was never time for gallivanting around the farm. Dad wanted me to come up on the back of the motorbike once. That was – oh, I can't remember. I wish I had.' She points. 'What's that?' She puts her glasses back on.

It takes me a while to see it. A sheep near the bottom of the hill, lying against a fence.

'Is it dead?' she asks.

It answers her question by kicking. We see the legs and body jerk, the head lift and fall back on the ground. 'No, just cast,' I say unnecessarily. 'We'll tell Erueti.'

'All it needs is for someone to roll it over on its feet,' she says, starting down the hill.

My legs ache. I don't want to go all the way down there for a big lump of fatty mutton. 'He'll come up on the four-wheeler. He'll attend to it. Diddy?'

'Come on,' she calls. 'I can't do it by myself.'

We lose the breeze and walk into the oven of midday sun. The track is harder downhill. Our shoes slip in the dry dirt and scuff dust over our jeans. A flock of sheep, spread across the hillside, stare at us and then run away, rear ends bobbing, dags rattling like castanets. The noise alarms the ewe lying against the fence. She kicks and bleats blah-blah sounds.

As we get closer, we realise that she's been there for some time. The grass has been worn away by her kicking and there's a spinach-coloured morass of droppings by her tail. She rolls her eyes at us, terrified.

'How are we going to do this?' says Diddy.

It isn't easy. The animal's back is downhill, pressed hard against the fence and we have to avoid her flailing hooves. We edge our way in, feeling the heavy heat of her wool, our nostrils full of the sharp smell of her fear. Her legs flail uselessly and she twists her neck, trying to see what we are doing. Blah-blah-blah.

Eventually we are wedged between her and the fence, her body pressed against our legs, the barbed wire at our back-sides as we bend over. We take a grip on her wool and heave. Blah-blah.

'Further down!' I tell Diddy. 'Let's get our hands under her.'

We try again and this time we roll the ewe upright. She's heavy, a dead weight against us. She doesn't know what to do with her legs. Just as I think that maybe she's too far gone, she kicks her feet, somehow gets them positioned, and stands up. We watch her limp down the hill to the river.

'I'll bet she's got a thirst,' I say.

Diddy brushes the legs of her pants and then puts her hands to her face. She sniffs, grimaces. 'I used to hate the lambing beat. I didn't mind the lambs but the process of acquiring them always seemed so messy and barbaric.'

The old ewe is now in the shade of the willows, drinking from a shallow ditch at the edge of the river. We turn and begin the journey up the hill. On the steeper parts I push my knees with my hands to make them work. Even Diddy stops regularly to admire the view.

'The hardest thing,' I say, 'was not having children. I wanted. A big family. Six or seven.'

'Bea! No!'

'Yes. I did. I couldn't. My tubes. They were blocked. Must have been. An infection. In those days. There was no.' I stop and straighten my back. 'Nothing they could do.'

'You were lucky to have Francis,' she says.

'He was. Beautiful. Such a lovely baby. I only wish.'

'That's another thing about the church,' she says. 'There's this assumption that if you're female, you're maternal.' She stops and wipes the perspiration off her face with the tail of her shirt. 'Some women are not mothers, just as some men are not warriors and hunters.'

I look back at the sheep which is still under the willows, still drinking. It's the same willow tree. All those years ago, Erueti and I in a mixture of light and shade, with water in the hollows where the cattle had trod and dragonflies electric blue on the watercress. He was so young and full of a knowing that burst through his innocence in an instant of loving. And we lived that summer by the river and no one ever discovered. And I never told. Never gave the memory away. I undo the backpack and take out the bottle of water which feels almost as warm as a teapot. There were buttercups there, too. He picked some for my hair.

'Do you want a drink?' I say, handing the bottle to Diddy.

'I find the nurturing image of women to be quite archaic,' she says. She drinks and wipes her mouth with the back of her hand. 'It's disturbing to think that people still subscribe to it.'

Erueti is pleased about the ewe. He gets some cold beer from the fridge and we sit in the kitchen, eating egg sandwiches and Afghan biscuits, drinking beer straight from the can although Donna has put out glasses.

'Where are you from, Donna?' asks Diddy.

'Ngapuhi,' Donna says.

'Where's that?'

'Diddy, it's not a place,' I tell her. 'Ngapuhi is Donna's tribe.'

'The Hokianga area,' Donna says. 'I go back two or three times a year, when I need it to get renewed. Did the shoes fit you all right?'

Erueti says, 'Donna calls my iwi Ngati Hau e Wha, tribe of the four winds. That's because I'm all mixed up, Ngati Arawa, Ngai Tahu, Ngati Porou.'

'And Italian,' says Donna.

'Sure,' says Erueti. 'And Italian.'

Diddy eats five egg sandwiches, straight off. She has always done this, fills up like a camel on some food that takes her fancy and then doesn't eat for the rest of the day.

'Where do you go next?' Donna asks.

'Wellington,' I tell her. 'Diddy and I need to spend some time going through the furniture and personal effects.'

Erueti nods slowly. 'Frank was a good man. They were

both good people. I got used to thinking about them like they were another set of parents.'

Donna says, 'It was a nice tangi, wasn't it?' She looks at Diddy. 'Funeral,' she says.

Diddy smiles. 'I know what a tangi is.'

'They are like our own people,' says Erueti. 'They will always be here with us.'

She did ask me if she could hear the tape I played for Dad the night before he died. I have it in my purse and on the drive to Wellington, I put it in the cassette player. She listens for a while, leaning forward in her seat. We don't talk. It's just the music, piano pieces with little clicks in between where I've taped. Got them from different. Well I think she's interested but then she puts her jacket against the door and her head. And she closes her eyes. I keep glancing at her. She looks young. It's her expressions that make her old, sort of monkey-faced. Asleep her face is. Dad looked like that in the funeral home. Years younger. She's thin. Her hair's grey. Apart from that she could be eighteen. I turn the music down.

'Leave it,' she says, without opening her eyes.

'I thought you were asleep.'

'No. I was listening.'

At the end of the tape she sits up and says, 'Well, what's the next topic of conversation? The Kiwiana restaurant?'

'You said you would tell me about your dressing gown.'

She frowns. 'I did?'

'I think it was Italian.'

Her face clears and she laughs. 'The story of my beautiful Venetian robe. That's some tale. You know how Dad was with money and possessions? I'm a little that way. I'm not profligate in spending but what I have means something. Right? Right. So the summer I went to Italy I bought just one thing for myself. It was a brocade robe that shimmered like a peacock's tail and I spent every cent I had on it. Oh, it was just gorgeous. For me it was the culmination of an Italian experience which had begun, I guess, with listening to Erueti's mother. Remember how she used to talk about Venice?'

'She'd clasp her hands and say it was the most beautiful city in the world.'

'It is, too. And this was the most beautiful robe in the world. I took it back to New York in my hand luggage as though I was carrying the Holy Grail. Now, at this time, Lal and his partner Byron were running the bookbinding venture from the apartment and we had –'

'Wait!' I put my hand out to stop her. I think I. The fragments of information and why she doesn't. 'Do you mean a business partnership? Or do you mean?'

'Both,' she says.

I don't know what to. Oh, that sun. It's low on the horizon and I need to adjust the visor. Just a bit. She is looking at me.

'Bea, I thought you knew. Lal is gay.'

'Well you said. About wine you said. When he drank more than one glass. You told me he snored.'

'He does, too.'

'So I assumed. It's natural to assume.'

'Yes, we sometimes do sleep together. You know – sleep?'

'I don't understand.'

She draws her feet up under her and curls up in the seat smiling. Then she pats me on the arm. 'Oh Bea, you should know by now. The only thing to understand in life is that there is no such thing as normal.'

9
1953

That Saturday morning, Delia was set to go to the skating rink with Celia Upton whose parents had a large tent in the camping ground behind the beach store. Celia was thirteen and she had breasts. Delia hoped that when she turned thirteen her chest would grow although there were no signs yet. Bea told her that Mum had met Aunty Em in town and Aunty Em had said, 'Is Delia developing?' According to Bea, Mum had replied, 'No. Flat as an ironing board.' Ironing board! Huh! Well, at least she didn't have really big ones that flopped when she ran. That looked disgusting. There was a joke whispered at school when the nuns weren't listening. 'What's the difference between a sweater girl and a Singer sewing machine? The sewing machine has got only one bobbin.' Anyway, Delia didn't care what people said about her flatness. Uncle Jack had told her she was already smashingly beautiful and all she needed was a few years to round her out.

Celia Upton had already rounded out. Celia Upton wore low-cut peasant blouses and gipsy hoop earrings and full skirts with ruffled petticoats. She had a short blue skating dress with matching gorgeous gussie pants and wooden

Hamaco skates on white competition boots. Celia Upton was worldly. That's what Mum said. Worldly. The word thrilled Delia. It covered a huge range of possibilities, some known, most unknown. It reminded Delia of the *True Romance* magazines where a man kissed a woman and took her into the back seat of the car, then, ten minutes later, they were driving home. The word 'worldly' was like that ten minutes, a deep crevasse that filled her with fascination and fear.

It was not possible for Delia to tell her mother that she had arranged to go skating with Celia Upton, so her excuse sounded weak. 'I hate surfing,' she said. 'I want to skate.'

'Bea can't go surfing on her own,' her mother said.

'Well, I'm not taking her.'

In the background Bea was blubbering, 'It's not fair! She always goes skating.'

'You're going surfing,' Mum said to Delia.

Delia went outside and sat at the picnic table, ready to develop a headache or a pain in her stomach. It was Uncle Jack who sorted things out. 'I'm in a spot of bother, kiddo,' he said. 'The tide is right for flounder. But you see, I half-pie promised to take young Bea surfing. I can't be helping your Dad with the net and watching out for Bea at the same time. I need a stand-in.' He put one of his stinky cigarettes in his mouth and struck a match. The blue in the flame was like the blue of his eyes. 'You reckon you can manage the deep end of the net?' he said.

'I'll take Bea surfing,' she said.

With so much to carry, they decided to take the car, putting the net in the boot and fastening the surfboards on the roof with ropes that went inside through the windows. Delia sat in the car, watching Uncle Jack reach up to tie knots in the ropes on the roof. His chest was a sandy brown colour with freckles and ginger hairs. If she moved her hand six inches she could tickle him under the arm. She said, 'Uncle Jack, will you take me skating this afternoon?'

He put his head down in the window space. 'Can't skate,' he said. 'But I'll come and watch my chick-a-biddy.'

'And me!' cried Bea, leaning across Delia. 'Watch me too, Uncle Jack!'

'Too right!' said Uncle Jack, going back to his rope.

That'll be the day, thought Delia and she stuck her elbow into Bea.

'Ow! Dad? Diddy punched me with her elbow.'

'You were squashing me,' said Delia.

There was a wind on the beach matching the energy of the waves which rose like green glass where the light caught them and then toppled into whiteness, bits of foam tossed back into the air. There was a fullness of noise too, the boom of the breakers, the rush against the beach, the raking back over white shells. Dad and Uncle Jack were making jokes about who would be on the deep end of the net but everyone knew it would be Uncle Jack because he was the tallest. 'What a bugger!' he said. 'I'll end up back in bloody Australia.'

Mum stayed in the car with the windows open to keep cool. She dressed for the beach the way she dressed for town, except that she didn't wear stockings. Her pink frock and bolero were newly ironed and the white sandals were the ones she had bought at Christmas. She wore lipstick and little pats of rouge on each cheek and 4711 eau de Cologne on her handkerchief tucked down her brassiere. As Dad often reminded the girls, their mother was a nifty dresser. When she came to the beach she brought a book with her. It was always the same book about the history of the Marists in the South Pacific and Delia was sure that her mother never read more than a few lines at a time. The book was simply there so that she didn't have to talk to people who walked past with their children or dogs.

Delia and Bea helped Uncle Jack and Dad to lay the long string net out on the beach. There were floats on the top of the net, lead weights at the bottom and poles that had to be put in each end. When you were dragging the net through the sea, you had to keep the bottom end of the pole firmly on the sand or the fish would escape. It was hard work and Delia was glad she wasn't doing it.

Dad and Uncle Jack were always joking around and having pretend fights. Before they even got the net into the water. Uncle Jack was having Dad on about not getting wet on the shallow end and next thing they were splashing each other and rolling around in the waves, shouting. Bea rushed in and jumped on top of them. Typical Bea. Delia yelled at her to help with the surfboards.

The wooden boards were really heavy. Dad had cut them from pine eighteen inches wide and five feet long, with a rounded shape at one end and a groove at the other to fit your waist. If the board got away from you on a breaker and you crashed into it, you could get blue bruises on your ribs. You had to be careful. Delia told Bea how important it was to hang on tight and not to go out too deep. Bea already knew those things but sometimes she forgot and then it was Delia who got into trouble.

They went into the sea behind the men, so the boards wouldn't scare the fish or get caught in the net, and Delia helped Bea catch her first wave. They were only knee deep and the wave had broken way out, but it still came rushing in with a lot of push. Delia held Bea against the board until the little white wall was at Bea's heels, then she let her go. The foam arched around Bea's shoulders and drove her before it, right up the beach, then left her, screaming with pleasure on the wet sand.

It was Delia's turn. She fitted the groove of the board just above her hip bones and as a wave broke behind her, she poised to leap. It was a fizzer. The board rose up and fell again, and the wave went on without her.

'I went farther than you!' Bea cried, as she dragged her board back.

'I'm not used to surfing in shallow water,' said Delia. 'But with you here, I don't have much choice, do I?'

'I went right up the beach,' said Bea.

'That was a fluke,' Delia said. 'Out deep just about every wave is a good wave. These are just stupid little waves for kids who can't swim.' She saw Bea's face get that blubbery look and she said, 'You did a good job holding the board.'

The men were moving away from them and now at a distance. Dad was in water that went from his waist to his knees. Uncle Jack, much deeper, had to rise up in a swell which meant that he was bringing the bottom of the net pole off the sand. Dad always saiolyou let the fish out when you did that. Did he tell Uncle Jack?

'Have a race,' said Bea, her board ready.

There were several cars on the beach now, all in a line on the firm sand by the high-tide mark. One man was putting driftwood into a trailer. Further along, there were three children and a dog digging in the sand at the water's edge. The wind made the view in every direction misty with spray.

'Here's one!' Bea shouted.

'No! That's no good either. Wait!'

Eventually they got a wave that took them into the shallows, where they grounded together, their knees scraping on bits of shell, and sand filling the legs of their swimsuits.

'I'm so good at surfing!' Bea screamed towards the beach, but there was no one to hear her.

They caught several more waves and then Delia noticed that the men were dragging the net in a big half-moon towards the shore. Uncle Jack had come around into shallow water and even from this distance, they could make out the top of the net moving up and down with the swell.

'I bet they got lots of flounder,' said Bea.

Delia put her hands on her hips. 'I bet they didn't get any. I saw Uncle Jack lifting his pole off the bottom. When you do that, all the fish swim out under the net.'

'No, they don't,' said Bea.

'Yes, they do.'

'Don't, don't, don't.'

'Do, do, do, do, do, do!'

The men were now out of the water, backs bent over the poles that were furrowing the wet sand. The net ropes pulled against them and behind the line of floats that curved in the shallow water, Delia saw splashing.

'We've got some!' she cried, and she waded, trailing her board. She dropped the board on the damp sand and ran, yelling, 'We've got some fish! We've got some fish!'

By the time she got to Dad and Uncle Jack, several people had stopped to look at the net coming out of the sea. It was alive with flapping. You could hear the slap, slap, slap of flounder tails above the noise of the wind and waves and voices.

Dad and Uncle Jack didn't make a big fuss the way they had the day before when they got just two flounder. Maybe it was because there were people watching. They dropped the poles and walked along the net. Delia went with them, touching her foot on the dark grey fish which were jumping about, coating themselves with sand.

'What do you reckon, Jack?' Dad said.

'About three dozen, I'd say, Frank,' said Uncle Jack. 'I don't know what we're going to put them in.'

'There's the sack we keep the net in,' said Dad.

Uncle Jack scratched his head. 'You think it's bloody big enough?'

They were talking like that when they all heard the screaming. Mum was half way down the beach, running towards them, waving her arms and shrieking something that Delia first thought was excitement over the fish. Uncle Jack looked quickly at Delia and said, 'Where's Bea?'

Where was Bea? Delia turned, expecting her sister to be behind her. She wasn't. Nor was she in the water where they had been surfing. That meant she had to be on the beach. Somewhere.

Mum was closer, pointing and screaming, 'Bea! Bea!' and Uncle Jack was running with high steps through the water. Then he dived into a wave.

Delia ran back to the place where she had left her surfboard, and shaded her eyes. She was bewildered by the fuss. Bea was all right. Bea was always all right. She just did things to get attention.

Uncle Jack was out there swimming, his arms making fast triangles through the water. Much closer, in the shallows, Bea's surfboard was bobbing up and down by itself. Delia waited for Bea to appear beside it.

There was no one at the net. The group of people had moved and now were gathered around Delia, some on the shore, others wading out into the water. Mum was crying, high-pitched sobs, and Dad was holding onto her.

'There she is!' someone yelled.

For an instant Delia saw her sister rising on a wave, face down, her arms and legs spread like a starfish.

A man and a woman waded deeper into the water, yelling and pointing but when a big wave came towards them, they walked backwards.

'He's got her,' the man said.

Delia saw Uncle Jack, then she didn't see him. He was swimming on his side with his upper arm tucked around Bea's chin. They would go through the top of a wave, down the other side and then disappear until the next wave bore them up. Dad left Mum and walked out to his shoulders, his arms held up to Uncle Jack. In a moment they were wading in with Bea held face down between them. She was all right. Her mouth had gone a blue colour but she was coughing up trickles of water and beginning to cry.

'Praise God!' Mum said.

Delia thought they would lie Bea on the sand and pump out her chest the way lifesavers did, but Uncle Jack just grabbed her around the middle and tipped her upside down. A lot more water came out of her mouth and nose and she struggled, making choking noises. Uncle Jack was gasping himself, but he carried her like that up the beach, followed by Mum and Dad. Then Uncle Jack sat on the sand and laid Bea, face down over his knees. He put one hand under her chin and neck while he stroked her wet hair with the other.

'You're all right, Buzzy Bea. You're all right.' His words came out funny because his chest was heaving for breath. 'You're a brave girl, little Buzzy Bea.'

In a few minutes Bea's face had got back its pink colour and she was crying. Uncle Jack handed her to Mum, who was sitting on the sand beside him and Mum held Bea's wet sandy head against her pink jacket. She looked up at Delia. 'I trusted you!' she said.

Delia glanced quickly around her, at Uncle Jack, at the people who stood watching.

Mum's face was pale, her mouth as thin as a bit of string. Her fingers spread around Bea's head as she stared over them at Delia, 'You left her to drown!'

'The kid's okay. That's all that matters,' said a man.

Uncle Jack slowly stood up. 'It was an accident,' he said.

'She knew!' Mum said at Delia. 'She didn't want to look after her sister. She argued!'

Delia tried not to cry but the tears came up by themselves and tipped out of her eyes. It was Dad who put his arm around her shoulders. 'Diddy was helping us,' he said. 'She thought Bea was with her.'

People were now moving away and Bea had her arms around Mum's neck. Mum said, 'Bea can you stand up?'

Crying and coughing, Bea shook her head.

'Try,' said Mum. 'Just see if you can stand up by yourself.'

Bea shook her head again and burrowed into Mum. 'My head hurts,' she said in a croaky voice. 'I feel sick.'

'Just as far as the car,' said Mum.

'Give her to me,' said Uncle Jack. 'I'll carry her back to camp.'

'No, Jack,' said Mum. 'You've already done enough. If it hadn't been for –' She stopped when Bea held out her arms to Uncle Jack.

'That's what Uncle Jacks are for,' he said, scooping Bea up high so that she was lying over his shoulder. At once she stopped crying and coughing and closed her eyes, her thumb in her mouth.

'She can go in the car,' Mum said.

'No. Jack's right. She should go back,' said Dad. 'You and Jack take her to the caravan. Diddy'll help me with the net.' He ruffled Delia's hair. 'We got a sackful of flounder to look after and it'll take a bit of doing, won't it Diddy?'

Delia nodded but didn't speak. More than anything she wanted her mother to make things right by telling her that it wasn't her fault, that she hadn't left Bea to drown, but Mum didn't say anything. She just turned, eyes down, and followed Uncle Jack up the beach.

Dad tried to make up for it by saying it was a good thing Bea'd had a scare. She was too impulsive, said Dad. A fright would make her think twice about taking risks. That didn't help Delia because it made her remember what she'd said to Bea about the best waves being in deep water, the shallows being for little kids. If Bea told Mum that, Delia would be in deep water, right enough.

She held the net sack open while Dad put the fish in it. They had caught thirty-three flounder, five crabs which Dad threw back, and two gurnard fish which looked like butterflies with beautiful wings. Not bad for one haul, said Dad. They folded the net over the two poles and carried it up to the car. Then Dad said there was really no place at the camping ground to clean a big haul of fish and wouldn't it be a good idea if they gutted them by the sea? They could use one of the surfboards as long as they gave it a wash afterwards. So with Dad dragging the sand-encrusted sack and Delia hauling a surfboard, they went back to the water's edge. Delia dug a hole in the wet sand and let it fill up. Dad took the flounder one by one out of the sack and held them flapping on the board while he cut a gash below their gills and squeezed the gut out. They were still wriggling when Delia washed them and put them back in the sack.

As she was getting into the car, she saw Mum's book lying open in the sand, its pages bent back. Mum must have dropped it in her hurry to call for help. Again, Delia got that bad feeling at the bottom of her stomach. By now Bea would have recovered enough to be telling tales.

When they drove up beside the caravan, Uncle Jack came down the steps and stood by the car, his hands in his pockets. 'She's right as rain,' he said to Dad.

Dad grinned as he got out. 'You're a good one, Jack,' he said.

'Hell, Frank,' said Uncle Jack and he started untying the surfboards.

Dad put eight flounder in a bucket and told Delia to take them inside for lunch. She didn't want to go in the caravan but it was all right because Mum had got over her bad mood and Bea was asleep, curled up with her Marigold doll. The frying-pan was already on the stove, crackling and spitting, and Mum was decorating the top of a salad with hard-boiled eggs.

'I didn't tell her to go into deep water,' Delia said. 'It wasn't my fault.'

Mum smiled and leaned towards her. 'I know, Diddy. She was running after you and she fell over. A wave dragged her out.'

'Oh.' Delia felt suddenly as light as a feather. 'Gosh! Little kids can be so stupid. I've told her not to run in the waves.'

Mum touched Delia's nose with the flat of a knife blade. 'Don't say gosh,' she said but she was still smiling.

'Is she all right?'

'She vomited a couple of times but Jack bought her some lemonade and she kept that down. I'm sure she'll be fine when she wakes up. We're going to take her to the doctor this afternoon. Just in case she's still got some water in her lungs.'

Delia lifted two flounder out of the bucket. Their bulgy eyes swivelled on the top of their heads and even though they were gutted, they jumped about. 'Uncle Jack's taking me skating this afternoon,' she told her.

'Do you want a flounder?' she asked.

'Ew! No!'

She laughed. 'I thought as much.' She lifted up a fish and put it straight into a dish of flour where it turned into a ghost. 'I think we're all going into Foxton,' she said, 'Uncle Jack included.'

Delia took a breath to say something, then closed her mouth and ran down the steps just as the first flounder hit the hot fat.

There were far too many flounder for one family. Dad and Uncle Jack took them around the campsite and gave them to people, including Mr Ewing, who had the beach store and the house next to it.

Mr Ewing looked at Delia. 'Is this the kiddy who got into difficulty this morning?'

'Nah!' said Uncle Jack. 'This young lady can swim like a dolphin. It was her little sister. She's okay now.'

'You have to watch that undertow,' Mr Ewing said. 'Nice fish. Are you doing anything tonight?'

Uncle Jack and Dad looked at each other.

'There's a party on at the house,' said Mr Ewing. 'Just the usual Saturday night affair. Men bring a bottle, ladies bring a plate. Kids welcome too. We just sit around, have a few beers and a bit of a singalong around the piano.'

'You got a piano!' said Uncle Jack. 'Did you know his missus is a pianist?'

'No kidding!' said Mr Ewing.

'She plays classical music,' Dad said.

'All that bloody fancy stuff,' laughed Uncle Jack. 'But she can play anything, mate. She can make a piano talk French or bloody Japanese, if you like. She's a cracker.'

Delia took a couple of steps backwards. Just as her

mother was being nice to Uncle Jack for rescuing Bea, he had to say something like that. If Mum heard about it, she wouldn't speak another word to him for the rest of the holidays, and that was a fact.

Mum didn't hear about it. That afternoon, Uncle Jack didn't say anything to tease her and she was more relaxed than she had been all holiday. She held onto Dad's arm and laughed a lot and Delia thought how pretty she looked when she was happy. They were all happy. Every now and then Delia wondered what would have happened if Uncle Jack hadn't been such a good swimmer or if Bea had sunk to the bottom and he hadn't found her. When those thoughts came into her head, she said something nice to Bea. She gave her a shilling from her pocket money and told her she would teach her to skate. Bea too, was different. She didn't show off. She didn't cry or whine. On the trip to Foxton they all sang 'Old McDonald had a Farm' and they took turns at being the animals.

The doctor said Bea was a very lucky little girl. He washed her ears out in case she got an infection in them but said she was the picture of health and he couldn't find a thing wrong with her. When Mum reported that to Uncle Jack, Dad and Delia, Uncle Jack thought there should be a celebration. They drove down the main street of Foxton, parked outside the milk bar, and he treated them all to peach melbas. They weren't kids' size, either. Each dish had three scoops of ice-cream, sliced peaches, whipped cream and pink wafer biscuits and Bea proved she was her old self by eating every last bit of juice.

Uncle Jack said to the girls, 'You can put your glad rags on tonight. We're going to a party.'

Dad looked at Mum. He hadn't told her.

'Party?' Mum said.

'The bloke who runs the store,' said Uncle Jack. 'Personal invite for the whole family. I think it's just their usual Saturday night shindig.'

'He's asked all of us?' said Mum. She put her hand on Dad's arm.

'What do you think?' Dad said.

She shrugged and smiled, her head close to his shoulder. 'It might be all right,' she said.

Delia couldn't believe that Mum had said that, this mother who avoided strangers and even people she knew.

Dad laughed in a pleased voice. 'We'll go then,' he said, squeezing Mum's hand. 'We'll have a good time.'

'We might as well get a few supplies while we're here,' said Uncle Jack.

'Supplies?' said Mum.

'Grog,' said Uncle Jack.

Mum carried a dish of pikelets in one hand and in the other, a plate of hard-boiled eggs filled with curry and onion. Uncle Jack and Dad had brown-paper bags that clinked when they walked. Delia and Bea ran ahead in their best dresses, Delia's made of pink everglaze and Bea's a bright yellow seersucker with broderie anglaise trim. Bea had on long white socks and lace-ups. Delia wore no socks at all and hoped that her legs were brown enough to look as though she had on seamless nylons. She hadn't been to a grown-up party before. She had rubbed her lips to make them pink and put some of Mum's perfume down the front of her dress, because it was better than nothing. No one else's mother wore 4711. Other mothers had real perfumes like Pink Mimosa or Evening in Paris or Californian Poppy.

There were already a lot of people from the camping ground at the house. When they went in, Mr Ewing opened the door to the living room and told them to put their bottles and plates on the table. He said that he didn't allow anyone else to touch his new stereogram but if they liked they could choose a long-playing record and he would play it for them. Dad had heard about long-playing records but he hadn't seen any before. He and Uncle Jack bent over the collection and after a lot of discussion, Uncle Jack came up with Bob Crosby and his Bobcats while Dad chose Perry Como. Perry Como came first. Delia sat in a chair and swung her legs while Dad sat on the couch next to Mum, holding her hand, and Uncle Jack poured some drinks. He and Dad had beers. Mum got a glass with some brown stuff and a bit of lemon on top.

'What is it?' she asked, sniffing.

'Pimms,' said Uncle Jack. 'A lady's drink.'

She sipped, screwed up her face and shuddered, then put the glass on the table.

Delia thought that Uncle Jack might say something but he just laughed. They all did.

The sun was coming in soft through the pine trees, no longer bright enough to light the room. Someone switched on a fluorescent light which flickered and flickered and then filled the room with a hard whiteness. Bob Crosby was playing now and several grown-ups were dancing. Uncle Jack, Mum and Dad stayed on the couch and by now Mum was sipping the drink and laughing at their jokes. Delia thought it was a good thing that Bea had nearly drowned. It had made everyone glad they were alive.

Bea went outside with the little kids. News had got around really fast. When Delia went out, the kids were still asking Bea questions. Did she go unconscious? Did she see her whole life passing before her eyes? What was it like to get your lungs full of salt water? Did the sea get into her brain? Bea kept saying she couldn't remember much, but they still asked her dumb questions. In the end they got sick of it and someone suggested they play ghosts. The idea was that you ran around the house, jumped up at a window and yelled, 'Boo!' If you scared a grown-up you got the ghost of the year award.

It was a childish game and Delia refused to play it. Instead she sat on the Ewing's front porch, watching the moths that flew in with dusk, wondering where the big kids were. The sky had that tint of green which comes before true darkness and somewhere, invisible, was the smoke from a wood fire mixed up with the smell of sausages. That was something they hadn't done yet this holiday, had a fire on the beach, burned driftwood down to embers, cooked potatoes and sausages and told spooky stories with firelight on their faces and darkness at their backs.

Bea came onto the porch and sat beside her. 'I've got a sore head,' she said, putting her hand to her forehead.

Delia didn't know if it was true, or if Bea had simply run out of attention.

'My brain hurts,' said Bea. 'I think I've got water in it. Can I stay here with you?'

'I'm going for a walk.' Delia stood up.

'Good,' said Bea firmly and stood, too, putting out her hand to be held.

Down the road a bit, there were wolf whistles, the squeal of bicycle brakes and boys' half-broken voices, throwing taunts. This is where the big kids were. The boys were in the middle of the road, horsing around on their bikes and teasing a group of girls who sat on the boards outside Mr Ewing's shop. The girls teased back, laughing, putting their hands over their mouths, touching their hair and leaning together when someone said something particularly funny or shocking. Celia Upton was not with them.

Delia pulled Bea by the hand. This was no place for little kids, she told her, and she marched her around the back of the shop, in the direction of the house.

'I don't want to play ghosts,' Bea said.

'Then you can go in the house with Mum and Dad and Uncle Jack.'

'That's boring. Why can't we stay out there?'

'It's for big kids only,' Delia said.

'That's not fair!'

'Don't whine!'

They were walking past the storeroom at the back of the shop, when Delia saw Celia Upton. She was against the wall and there was a boy pressing against her. They were kissing.

Bea stopped, her eyes and mouth all of a roundness. Delia yanked her arm so hard that she nearly fell over.

'That's Celia Upton!' Bea's whisper was high-pitched.

'Will you hurry up?'

Bea ran and stumbled. 'Did you see, Diddy? Did you see that boy's hand?'

'No, I didn't!'

'He was being rude,' she said, her voice half laughing, half scared.

'You shouldn't have looked!' Delia snapped. 'I thought you had a headache.'

They were now back at Mr Ewing's house, which was full of light and talk and music. The little kids were still running around, booing at the windows.

'You like Celia Upton,' said Bea. 'Celia Upton is your friend.'

'No, she isn't!' Delia said. 'Celia Upton is –' She looked for a suitable word, could not find it. 'Celia Upton is worldly,' she said.

Mr Ewing's house was full of people, most of them

grown-ups, and the air was thick with cigarette smoke. The noise was terribly loud, with everyone laughing and shouting and the stereogram turned up on 'Cherry Pink and Apple Blossom White'. Delia pushed through the crowd, dragging Bea, and they both got beer spilled on them.

Uncle Jack, Mum and Dad were still on the living room couch. Dad had his arm across the back of the couch behind Mum's shoulders. Uncle Jack had his arm on top of Dad's. In their other hands they held bottles of beer. Mum, in the middle, had both hands in her lap around a glass. She was laughing a lot and there were two pink spots on her cheeks.

Delia pushed Bea in front of Mum and said, 'She's got a headache.'

Mum went on laughing.

'Bea's got a headache!' Delia yelled.

'Gidday, kiddo. Gidday Buzzy Bea!' Uncle Jack raised his bottle to them. 'Having a good time?'

At once Bea lunged at Uncle Jack and tried to get on his knee.

'Bea has got a headache!' Delia shouted it as loud as she could.

'It's got better,' said Bea, leaning over Uncle Jack's knee. She looked at Delia. 'The water came out.'

Delia said to her mother, 'I think we should go,' but her mother didn't move. She went on laughing, although no one had said anything funny and her eyes were strange, kind of wet and slow. Then Delia realised what it was. Her mother was drunk. Delia Munro's mother who never had anything stronger than half a glass of beer topped up with lemonade, was just like those people you saw coming out of the pub at six o'clock. Dad and Uncle Jack were no better, but it was different for them. They were men.

Delia took the glass from her mother and put it on the

table. She grabbed her mother's hands and pulled. 'I want to go home. Mum? Mum? I want to go back to the caravan.'

About then the music stopped and someone started banging on a bottle with a spoon. The talking noise dropped until the clang of the bottle filled the room. Mr Ewing called out, 'Attention, ladies and gentlemen. Attention, please. We have in our midst a real pianist. Where is she?'

'He means you, lamb chop,' said Uncle Jack.

Mum laughed and shook her head.

'Where is our pianist?' called Mr Ewing.

Dad stood up, 'Come on sweetheart.'

'Sock it to them,' said Uncle Jack.

Mum went on laughing and shaking her head but she stood up. People moved back and in a moment there was a clear path between Mum and a small cottage piano on the far wall.

'Here she comes,' said Mr Ewing. 'Let's give our resident pianist a big hand.'

Mum stood wobbling on her high heels, as people clapped. She took a couple of steps as though the floor were uneven and then reached out to Dad and Uncle Jack who came up on either side of her. They guided her over to the piano and pulled out the music stool. She sat down, swaying, and Delia thought she might fall off.

'Play the old moonbeam,' said Dad.

'By the light of the silvery moon,' said Mr Ewing.

'No sirree!' Dad wagged his finger at Mr Ewing. 'The other one. You know, the "Moonlight".'

'How about "Black and White Rag"?' said Uncle Jack. 'You learned that yet?'

Mum looked at Dad and Uncle Jack. Then she held onto the edge of the piano, to look back at Bea and Delia. 'I am going,' she said, 'to play for Beatrice. She got drowned.

Nearly. I am going to play for Bea.' Then she turned back to the piano and rubbed her hands together.

Delia knew what she meant, 'The Flight of the Bumble Bee' by Rimsky-Korsakov. Sometimes at home, Bea sat on the edge of the piano stool while Mum's nimble little fingers whizzed in a buzzing whirl up and down the keys. Mum said that it was Bea's tune and that it was really hard to play.

Delia moved closer and touched Mum on the shoulder. 'Let's go back to the caravan,' she pleaded.

Mum took absolutely no notice. She put out one finger and stabbed a note. There was silence in the room. She lifted her hand and stabbed another note, leaning over the keyboard to look at her finger from all angles. Then she played a third note. There was a restless movement in the crowd and someone laughed with embarrassment. Delia pulled at her mother's shoulder. 'Please, Mum. Let's go. Let's go.'

Mum swung round on the piano stool and smiled at Dad and Uncle Jack who smiled back at her as though there wasn't a thing wrong in the whole wide world. Talk broke out, a quick buzz of conversation and people moved towards each other and their glasses.

Delia wanted to fall down and die. 'Let's go!' she cried.

Slowly, Mum turned back to the piano. She held her hands out in front of her, turned them over and looked at them as though seeing them for the first time, then she brought them down on the keys.

She was playing it. Oh, she was playing it! The conversation stopped as though it had been chopped off by an axe and everyone pressed forward to look. It was 'The Flight of the Bumble Bee' and she was playing it so fast, her fingers were a blur. Up and down the keyboard, buzzy, buzzy, buzzy, went those little hard hands hitting at such speed that the notes all fell on top of each other and ears couldn't keep up. Her shoulders and arms danced along with her hands, up and down, up and down, and Uncle Jack lifted the lid of the piano to let out more sound. Buzzy, buzzy, buzzy. Zoom, zoom. People's mouths were hanging open. Only Dad and Uncle Jack still laughed. But oh, she had never played it this fast before. There was a whole hive of bees racing around the room with frantic little engines, circling heads, diving on bottles and glasses, flying right through people and making holes in them that would last forever. Buzzy, buzzy.

She lifted her hands and it was over.

For a second no one did anything. Then there was a storm of noise, shouting, clapping, stamping, whistles. As Mum stood Dad and Uncle Jack grabbed her and hoisted her up on their shoulders. They walked with her around the room and she had to keep her head down to stop hitting the ceiling. People moved out of their way, looking up, calling out compliments and clapping. Mum wasn't laughing now, just smiling politely, holding onto the collars of Dad's and Uncle Jack's shirts. They carried her to the door and then dropped her down.

'More! More!' people were shouting.

But it was time to go home. Without a reply, they went outside, Mum in the middle, her arms across their backs, their arms over her shoulders and each other, Delia and Bea running to catch up.

Dad sang, 'You are my sunshine, my only sunshine.'

Mum and Uncle Jack joined in. 'You make me happy when skies are grey. You'll never know dear, how much I love you. Please don't take my sunshine away.'

That's how they walked back to the caravan, the three of them swaying and stumbling together and singing into the night. Delia grabbed Bea's hand and they swung their arms, joining in.

'The other night, dear, as I lay sleeping, I dreamed I held

you in my arms. But when I woke, dear, I was mistaken. So I hung my head and cried.'

A moon had come up over the pine trees, like a rocking horse, and the air was full of little white moths which could have been bumble bees if the moon had been the sun.

'You are my sunshine, my only sunshine. You make me happy when skies are grey.'

At the caravan, Uncle Jack said goodnight and went off through the trees to his tent. Mum and Dad laughed and kissed and pulled Delia and Bea close in a hug. The air was warm and in it Delia could still detect smoke and sausages. And beer. And sea. And pine trees. When she put her head back she could see the little moon caught in a net of branches.

'You'll never know, dear, how much I love you. Please don't take my sunshine away.'

10
DELIA

I am both fascinated and frustrated by her singular point of view. For the past twenty miles she has been sketching character portraits of her son and daughter-in-law that are straight out of some comic book or B-grade movie. When I point this out to her, she says with perfect conviction, 'I suppose clichés exist because there are so many of them.'

There's not much you can say to a supposition like that.

This part of the Hutt Road is all new to me. Where did the miles of suburbia come from? What happened to the farms where we used to pick blackberries and mushrooms with Aunty Em? We come to the foreshore at Petone and I gasp at the spectacle of Wellington in a sunset, the sky above the hills bright orange, the dish of the harbour shimmering a dull tomato red.

Bea misses it because she is talking about Francis and Chloe. 'He asked me about pavlova and she deliberately. He wanted to know the three ways we served it. I didn't get a chance to tell him.'

She turns a corner towards the eastern bays and the blood-red sea glows at my right shoulder. Not quite. There is half a road between me and the beach. It makes me uncomfortable. I haven't readjusted to driving on the left side. 'Well tell me,' I say.

Bea glances in my direction.

'Tell me about your three pavlovas. I'm interested.'

She takes a deep breath. 'There's Mount Taranaki,' she says and her voice has gone from shrill to gruff. 'That's a peaked mound of pavlova baked over a peach stuffed with praline, topped with cream. Not fluff squirted from a can, either. We beat fresh dairy cream. Then we have Rotorua which is a three-layered pavlova with caramel in between. Are you really interested?'

'Yes, Bea, I am.'

'The third one is Ninety Mile Beach. It's flavoured with coriander and cardamon. It's served with a mixture of cream and chestnut puree.' She looks at me. 'They're my own recipes.'

'How's your new chef?'

'Good. Excellent, in fact.'

'What's his name?'

'Margaret. Mrs Margaret McDonald.' She smiles. 'I'm not sure McDonald is a good name for a chef with Cordon Bleu training.'

'Ah!' I lean back in the seat. 'Now I know why you no longer get your navel filled with liqueur.'

'Oh Diddy!'

'It was the only bright note at Mum's funeral, you and your chef.'

'I didn't tell you that at her funeral. Diddy, I didn't!'

'No. You told me before their golden jubilee dinner when you were pouring Cointreau on the *crêpe flambée*.'

'You remembered that?'

'Oh God, Bea. I remembered it over and over. That visit turned out so awful, I had to hang onto something funny. I thought of it during Mum's Mass. Your navel filled up with alcohol and this little kitten of a chef.'

'Yes,' she says. 'Lawson. He was lovely, really and truly lovely.'

'I thought his name was Rawson?'

She looks vague. 'Yes, you're right. Imagine you remembering that. It was Rawson. And he had this funny surname. Stockport. The kitchen staff called him Stockpot. You know, Diddy, he had just the loveliest hips. The bone and muscle sort of rolled when he walked. I could have watched. Have you noticed that? The way there will be one thing about a man that is utterly captivating? Like the shape of his knuckles? Or his ears?'

I laugh and shake my head.

'I once knew this man who had achondroplasia.'

'What's that?'

'Dwarfism. He was so lovely. He had a kind of heavy brow which made his eyes unbelievably intense. You know? They were compelling. You thought you could fall into them and never come out, they were so beautiful.'

'Bea, you are amazing! You really are!'

She dips the lights for an approaching car and says, 'I was thinking about Lal. Has he always been?'

'Yes.'

'Oh.' She puts the lights back up. 'Well what about? I mean.'

'No.' I tell her.

'You don't know what I was going to say.'

'Yes, I do. You were trying to ask me if I was homosexual. The answer is no. I'm not homosexual. I'm not heterosexual. I'm not anything sexual.'

'What about when you were younger?' she asks.

'The same.'

'I'm sorry, I just don't.'

I want to tell her to mind her own business but I say, 'Autoerotic is the word you're looking for.'

She looks flustered. 'Hasn't there ever been anyone?'

'No.'

'But what about being in love?'

I sit up straight. 'Bea, as far as I'm concerned, sex has nothing to do with love. Of course, I love people. I love lots of people.'

'You're obviously fond of Lal.'

'Lal and I love each other very deeply if you want to know, but it's got nothing to do with sex. I happen to think that love is about giving. Sex is a completely selfish act. As far as I'm concerned, it's not terribly important.'

'Oh no, Diddy, you can't say that. It's the most glorious. The total surrender to love.'

'Bullshit! It's just an occasional itch. And if that itch happens to be on my body, then I'm the one who knows best how to scratch it.'

'But Diddy!' She looks genuinely distressed and she holds her breath, a sign that she is thinking of something to say that will be meaningful and proper. I am rescued from it by synchronicity, her street appearing in front of the car and, just around the corner, close to the beach, her house.

What is it about wooden beach houses that makes them instantly recognisable from Cape Cod to California to Wellington? Even if you can't see the ocean you know it's there and you suspect that it comes up in the night to wrap invisible arms around clapboard walls, imprinting them with the smells of everything that has lived and died on the sea floor. The paint always has the same chipped look. The windowsills are always flaking. There are shells paths, geraniums and lavender and succulents, and bits of driftwood or a glass buoy by the porch. Tonight it's too dark to see the ocean but I can smell it everywhere.

Bea puts the key in the front door, opens it and turns on the light. I haul my baggage out of the trunk and go up the steps.

Beach houses all have the same smell inside, too, sundried wood, sunwarmed carpet, furniture oil, old photos lined up on ledges as salty as sea urchins.

Bea says, 'Leave your suitcase in the sitting room and come on through.' She is putting lights on in the kitchen. 'Kick off your shoes. Make yourself at home.'

It is as I would expect, a big and well-equipped kitchen although I don't know who she would entertain here. At the end of the sink bench there is a solid block table and four padded chairs. By the wall under the window, a couch is covered with books, papers, letters. Bea gathers them with a few quick movements and says, 'I left in a hurry. There wasn't time.'

'It's a nice house. How long have you had it?'

'Less than a year. It's lovely living so close to the sea. Well, sit down. Sit down. What would you like to eat?'

'I'm not hungry, Bea.'

'I'm starving. You have to eat something. Remember what Dad used to tell us? If an animal is thin, it's sick. Human beings are animals.'

'Thanks,' I say.

'I didn't mean you were too thin, Diddy.'

'Yes, you did.'

'I didn't.'

'You did, Bea. You said it.'

'I meant if you didn't eat you could get sick. What about an omelette with herbs and fresh Gruyère?'

'No thanks.' I pick up a magazine and put it down. 'Have you got any wine?'

'Yes. Wine. I've got. But it's not chilled, Diddy.'

'Doesn't matter. Where can I plug in my laptop?'

While she is busy finding a bottle and glasses, I check my e-mail, letters of reassurance from Momo and Sylvie. Is it only when I am there that things go wrong? There is also a note from Antwan bearing happy news.

I call out, 'Bea, Regus and Holly have had a baby boy.'

'Are they friends of yours?' she asks, struggling with a corkscrew and a bottle wedged between her knees.

'Regus is our flooring expert. I told you. He's been on maternity leave. They wanted to have a home birth.'

'It went well?'

'Yes, very well. Eight pounds two ounces. Bea, they've called him Munro.'

'They did? After you? That's lovely, Diddy. What a nice thing for them to do. How's Lal?'

'He says the snowploughs are out.'

'It's snowing?'

'Yep. Six inches in the last few hours.'

She brings me a glass. 'Munro,' she says. 'I've never heard it as a first name. It sounds quite manly, doesn't it? I suppose they'll be asking you to be godmother. Are they?'

'Baptists.'

'Oh. Well. It's a nice thing for them to do.' She puts her head on one side and says, 'They're like your family, aren't they? Lal and Aaron and whatsisname. Your gang.'

'Yes,' I say. 'I suppose they are a surrogate family.' I hold up my glass. 'Cheers, Bea. *Salud, amor y dinero*.'

She looks at me.

'It means health, love and money,' I explain.

She laughs, slapping her knee. 'I know what *amor* means. I thought you were saying, "Salute love and dinner." I thought you were saying you were hungry.'

She makes me an omelette and I eat it, well, most of it. I'm tired. Two glasses of wine and my body is reminding me that its clock is still set eight hours ahead.

'I'm ready for bed, Bea. I've done a lot of walking, had a lot of sun, rescued a sheep.'

'You're sleeping in my room,' she says. 'I'll have the spare bedroom.'

'No, no, no.' I stand up. 'The spare room will be fine.'

'You won't get into it. Truly, Diddy. There's so much stuff stored.'

'If you can get into it, I can get into it. Where is it?'

She pushes past me and leads the way through the lounge. I see what she means. The room has a narrow divan against the wall nearest the door. The rest of the space is taken up with boxes and the grand piano covered with a quilt. I put my suitcase on the bed and with both hands lift back the thick fabric that covers the piano lid. Under it is Mum's old music stool.

The phone rings in the kitchen and Bea goes off to answer. I raise the piano lid and play a few arpeggios. The keys are still and so are my fingers. The sound is muffled by the cover. Three notes are badly off. I pull out the stool and look inside it for sheet music. There is a scant collection and I expect that her library of music has either gone or been packed in boxes. I find some Scriabin, a little Bach.

I hear Bea talking to someone. 'That's nice,' she says. 'That's really lovely.'

Ah, Handel's 'Largo', something at my level of accomplishment. I open the pages and rest them on the piano, aware that she was probably the last person to play the piece. I come close to smelling her perfume on it, the lightness of 4711.

I could not document the amount of musical experience that has been perfumed by 4711. Not all of it piano, either. In an auditorium, the woodwinds breathe the opening bars of Debussy's 'L'Après Midi d'une Faune' and at once the air is full of the old fragrance warmed by summer and a bass note of pine needles. I turn on Public Service radio and there is some unidentified Russian choral work, *a cappella*, perfect pitch, redolent with the same scent of pleasure and unease.

Once, a few years ago, I bought a bottle of 4711. In Cologne, actually. But poured from the bottle, it was something quite different.

I touch the first chord of Handel's 'Largo' and hear a note off-key. That's all right. With all the moves it has had, it's a wonder that the piano can be played at all. There are no missing felts. No broken strings. La-la-de-dah, dum-de-de. That sounded awful. I'm more rusty than the instrument. I turn the page. The light is poor. The last time I played this, I didn't have bifocals that broke up the staff and sent it wobbling down to the ledger lines.

I remember her little hands. Mine are big, an octave and two. She said that if I'd had the ear to go with them, I would have been brilliant. She wasn't putting me down. She never condemned or flattered anyone. She was making a statement of fact. How she would have loved to have had hands like mine which could have raked in the whole keyboard for her in a way her own would not, Rachmaninoff, Brahms, some of that expansive Chopin. Dum, dum, de-dum. Bea had her small hands but Bea's fingers hated the piano. And then there was my big span with no life, no soul in it. How painful that must have been for her. La-la-la-la. Mediocre *cum laude*. But even so, playing gives me great pleasure. I don't know why I haven't had a piano in New York.

I am attempting the 'Largo' for the second time when Bea comes in. 'That was Chloe,' she says. 'Ringing from Sydney.'

I turn quickly. 'Is everything okay?'

'Yes.' Bea looks puzzled. 'Francis was out with a client. Chloe said she was ringing to see if we'd got back all right. She thought I might want to speak to the children. It's seven o'clock over there. They were just going to bed.'

'Did you speak to them?'

'Yes.' Bea sits down on the bed, next to my suitcase. 'I don't know why she rang.'

I grin at her. 'Maybe guilty conscience,' I say.

Bea's face clears. 'You're probably right!'

'I was joking! Hey Bea, I didn't mean that! It was a bad attempt at sarcasm!'

'Many a true word is spoken in jest,' Bea says.

'Bea! I said I didn't mean it. She called you. She called you long distance. Doesn't it occur to you that she might be trying very hard to be nice?' I stop myself from adding something about Bea's attitude.

'Her problem,' says Bea, 'comes from the fact. She is so possessive of Frank. She won't let him do a thing without her say-so. I'm not going over there again, Diddy. My grand-children treat me like a guest. And Frank. You don't know what it's like to have a son who talks to you as though you were a charity case.'

I swing around on the piano stool and pretend to play a violin.

She stops mid-sentence, gives me a small smile and then goes out, tossing her head.

Great! I think to myself. Fantastically, flipping great!

* * *

I don't know what I have been dreaming but I wake up, clammy, agitated, with a terrible feeling of desolation. It is not associated with my parents but with my apartment back home, a sense of the thousands of miles between me and it, and no way of crossing them. It takes me some minutes to recollect that I have a plane ticket and that tomorrow I'll be leaving Auckland non-stop for Los Angeles. What was the dream that cut all my bridges? I don't know but as I lie in the narrow bed next to the piano, the trivia of my neighbourhood becomes very real and very dear and I count images like gold coins, Niki who sells flowers on the corner, the tail of his pet rat hanging out of his shirt pocket, Arly and Mike who still twirl pizza dough by hand, Rex our doorman whose diets never last more than a day, the woman who takes her labrador for a walk every night at seven, Johnny the panhandler who sometimes sits on our steps, rattling a styrofoam cup for his habit. 'God bless you, Delia. Praise Jesus for you, Delia.' I miss the blinking neon sign 'Kosher Chinese Restaurant', I miss the entire village of our building. I miss the Greenacre Park opposite where old men sit wrapping the *New York Times* around their early morning grumpiness. I miss the melted tar in summer, the ice in winter, the black garbage bags, the black umbrellas, the yellow taxi cabs, the sirens, the people noise, the whole steam and stink of it.

Yesterday in Napier I saw in a bookshop the latest *New Yorker*. It was two months old. Two goddam months! I felt as though I was falling off the end of the earth.

I miss Lal.

He'll be making lassi for his mother, mixing yoghurt with a little honey, a little salt, the way she likes it, pouring it over ice cubes while snowflakes immolate themselves on the warm stained glass of the living room windows and she, a little older, a little more blind, is trying to stitch yet another rug or pillow cover, pausing every few minutes to ask, 'When did you say Delia is coming back?'

The phone rings in the distance and I wait for Bea to answer it.

It is ridiculous to be so homesick that you want to exchange a New Zealand summer for a New York snowstorm.

The phone clicks but the voice is not Bea's. 'I'd like to leave a message for Delia Munro. This is Lal speaking. Could you tell her that I –'

I am out of bed and bumping into the piano stool. Wait! Wait! Running to the kitchen.

'– have arranged to meet her at Newark Airport. I've got the arrival time. Thank you.'

Wait! Wait! 'Hello Lal!'

'Delia! Well, hi sweetheart! I was just about to hang up!'

'It's great to hear your voice. Are you calling from the apartment?'

'No, the office. It's five after three. I was sitting here feeding some notes into the computer and I had this sudden urge to hear a funny New Zealand accent.'

'Lal, I don't know how you do it. You always know! It's morning here. I was half asleep. I forgot the time difference.' I look at the kitchen window and see the beach and sea. Bea is out there, talking to a man with a little dog. 'Lal, in this place they tell me I have an American accent.'

'Don't you believe it.' He says. 'Did you check your e-mail already?'

'Yes! Regus and Holly!'

'Munro, huh? What do you think of that?'

'I don't know what to say, Lal. I'm pleased and embarrassed. Have you seen him?'

'Oh sure! We all went over there with the usual cute stuff, polar bear T-shirts and stuffed toys. I took some flowers from you and me, both.'

'What does he look like? The baby?'

'I just saw his head. A bit like a large prune. Are you still flying in Friday? Good. I'll be there, somehow. The roads are so bad we've had to delay the Poughkeepsie job. Icestorms everywhere. I'll probably get a cab to the airport.'

'Thanks, Lal. Lal? Next time I bitch at you, will you remind me that I've missed you like hell?'

He laughs. 'Me too, sweetheart.' Then he says, 'I guess it hasn't been easy. Did you get to see the farm?'

I was about to hang up but now I pull over a chair and tell him all of it, the funeral, the farm, Bea's house, Bea and of course, the piano.

'Let's bring her over,' he says. 'Let's bring them both over.'

I find a towel, have a shower and am dressed before Bea comes in. She is bare-footed, large and beaming in a pink sarong, and her hair is wet.

'Just been for my morning swim,' she says. 'I did look in on you but you were fast asleep. Was the bed comfortable?'

'I saw you talking to someone.'

'That's the new neighbour. He's such a nice man. He's got this dear little dog that he takes. He's fifty-eight, born the same month as you.'

'Does he also have a dear little wife?'

'Oh Diddy, for goodness sake! I've only just met him. Did you manage the shower all right? You have to twiddle the thingy. I'm getting it fixed.'

'I didn't know you were a swimmer, Bea.'

'Didn't you? A kilometre every morning. In winter though, I go to the heated pool. Heck, I've swum for years.'

'I thought you were terrified of water.'

'I was. Half a lifetime ago. It was precisely that. So I took

178

swimming lessons. You see how much we've found out in just four days? Imagine a week!' She sees the red light on the answering machine and presses the playback button. Before I can say anything, Lal's voice comes into the room. 'I'd like to leave a message for Delia Munro. This is Lal speaking –'

'I heard it,' I tell her. 'I got to it.'

Bea resets the answering machine. 'Your last day,' she says. 'Your last day already. Well, that's the way it is. We'd better make the most of it.'

'Have you ever had a white Christmas?' I ask.

She looks quickly at me. 'What?'

'Lal suggested you come over next Christmas. It's a good idea. We'll take time off, maybe go up to the Finger Lakes, take you on a sleigh ride. You'd love it.'

She rubs the back of her neck and stares at the phone.

I tell her, 'Most New Zealanders never see past New York City. The state is so big, so beautiful. You know I saw a bear not seventy miles from Broadway? No kidding! It was up a tree raiding a bird feeder.' I stop. 'Well, I can't guarantee you a white Christmas but I can guarantee cold.'

She rubs her arms with the towel and says, 'I'd be scared of getting on your nerves.'

'Bea!'

'I do. I know I do, Diddy. We've always been oil and water.' She goes on rubbing. 'I'd like to come. Yes. I would really, really like.'

'Good. That's settled. Come for a month.'

'A month?'

'And don't change it to four days.' I give her a push. 'Oh go on, have your shower. Do you trust me to make the coffee?'

'I'd like to come for a month.' Her voice is so serious. 'Where would I stay?'

'We have a couch that folds down. Manorama doesn't like it. She thinks it'll swallow her in the middle of the night. But you'll manage. Oh, one other thing. Lal says yes to the piano.'

'What?'

'We'll snip the piano. God knows where we're going to put it even if we do get it into the elevator. I guess the legs unscrew. Anyway, he says it'll fit and that I should have it because its totemic.'

Bea clasps her hands. '*Deo gratis*! I get my spare room back! Diddy, I'm so glad. I don't know what it'll cost but if they can ship cars they can ship a piano.' She frowns. 'What on earth did he mean by totemic?'

I laugh. 'Bea, Lal is going to be an entirely new experience for you. I promise.'

'You are quite sure it's all right to stay for a whole?'

'Yes. You and I will fight but we'll get over it. And Bea, I'm not completely lost. I do go to Midnight Mass on Christmas Eve. It's a habit. Lal says he's not sure if it's my Catholic upbringing or my solstice instinct, but anyway, he comes too. You'll like St Patrick's Cathedral.'

But she is not impressed, I can tell, and I guess my tone has been too flippant.

She says, 'We could probably find a shipping firm today, I'd better have a shower and get dressed. There are all those boxes to go through. I have to ring the staff. I said I'd be away a week. We can't just go. Do you mind an early dinner so you can meet? Look around the place before it opens? Good. Yes, yes, you make the coffee.' And she disappears towards the bathroom, leaving me wondering how she ever runs a business.

Sorting the contents of the boxes is not as simple as I thought it would be. There is very little that I want, some old school reports, a few photos, but the process of going through the museum of their lives brings up a rawness that is not diminished by Bea's cheerful questions about New York. There is a packing case full of small, neat shoes, hardly worn. I didn't know Mum had so many. I didn't even know that she liked shoes this much. Then there is a cardigan I haven't seen before which must have belonged to Dad in later years. The elbows are out. The pockets sag. I hold it to my face and inhale the strong weed smell of his tobacco.

I say, 'I don't know about Father O'Donnell's broken heart theory. His strokes were probably caused by his smoking.'

'Probably,' she says. 'Are you quite sure about Christmas?'

'Don't ask me that again, Bea.'

'But a whole month?'

'Absolutely.' I drop the cardigan back in the box and pick up a crystal bowl. 'Has Francis seen his grandparents' things?'

'No. I said nobody until you. Well, there's Francis and Erueti and Donna and maybe. I must send a card to Chloe.' She looks at me. 'I was tired last night.'

'We have to be careful lest people live up to our expectations of them.' That is all I dare say on the subject. I put the bowl back. 'I really don't need any of this. What they don't take can go into the St Vincent de Paul shop. But I will ship all her music, if you don't want it. Lal suggests I have some more tutoring. It's not such a crazy idea.'

'How did you meet him?' she asks.

'Who? Lal? I don't remember. It was in our Greenwich Village days and there were mainly students in the building. I had a certain status among the penurious youth who were all younger than me. I was a graduate with a regular job. That meant something. There was a group of young gay men interested in music and theatre, on the same floor. They provided me with safe and agreeable escorts while I provided tickets. It was a very happy arrangement. At some stage I noticed a quiet man who walked as though he wanted to be invisible. I didn't know his ethnicity, thought he was probably Arab. There was nothing memorable.'

It is true. I don't know when we first spoke, saw the first movie, shared the first meal. Others came and went. His partners came and went. Years had passed before I grew into the realisation that he was the only person in my entire existence with whom I had discussed my deepest feelings. Years more would go by before we both realised that apart from one small section of our bodies, we shared something deep and enduring.

I tell all this to Bea. She says, 'How do you feel about his? You know, his partners?'

'What do you mean, how do I feel? He's not promiscuous and he's got good judgement. They've been fine people. I don't think there's been anyone for a couple of years. That's because of an attraction to a dead guru called Mahatma Gandhi. But that could change.'

'Don't you get jealous?' she asks.

'Jealous?' I start to laugh.

'Possessive,' she says.

'I was possessive about the Italian robe but that was different. Why should I be? Sure, I hate the idea of my body being invaded but I don't project that on other people.'

'You really are,' she says. 'Technically.'

'Yes.'

'What about? Tampons.'

'Nope. Pads and I'm past that.'

'How do you get on for smear tests?'

'Never had one.'

'Oh Diddy!'

'Virgins are low risk,' I tell her.

'I didn't know that,' she says, her face so very serious that I can't contain my laughter.

'Think of it, Bea. We represent the twin stereotypes of Catholic womanhood, virgin and Magdalene. Isn't that interesting?'

She decides, after all, to smile. 'It was nice of you not to say prostitute.'

'You could never be a prostitute,' I tell her. 'You could never charge.'

'That's right. I couldn't. Oh Diddy, I just couldn't. You know.' She sits on the bed beside me. 'I love men. I do. I just love everything about them and I hate hearing. When women put them down. They're so vulnerable. They pretend to be tough but. Sometimes I get the feeling I want to gather up all the men in the world and love them and love them. Can you understand that?'

'I don't relate to it personally, but I see it in you.' I realise that she's crying. 'It's your strength,' I say and then stop, confounded by the truth of the statement.

She picks up the corner of the bedspread to wipe her face. 'Thank you.' She smiles. 'It's funny, you know. Thinking about love. It's so huge in the heart. I remember Tony and it's like the only love there ever was. But then I feel the same about Barrie, about Erueti, Rawson, Pete. The same about them all. The memory of love. That doesn't change. Only their faces. I'm not talking about desire, Diddy. The feeling's a fullness, big, big. Sometimes I believe. It sounds stupid. That my heart could. No, not break. That's different. Burst. Yes, burst wide open.'

I put my hand on her shoulder. 'Actually, Bea, there are

no words to describe us and our relationships. Do you realise that? Women like us must be as old as humanity. We've been around for millions of years. Yet there is no language for the way we love.'

She nods and sighs. 'People like life to be tidy,' she says.

By mid-afternoon I have gone through all the photos and I have not found what I'm looking for. At one time there were dozens of snapshots, most of them taken with Dad's old Box Brownie but others too, pictures of them in the Air Force during World War II, with planes and cars, a heap of wedding photos which included the best man. Now I find just a sepia portrait of Mum and Dad as bride and groom, very young, very sober, and on their own. It seems that every image of Jack Holland has been destroyed.

11
BEATRICE

After a while I have to remind her. I love New Zealand and everything about. I love the clean air, the beaches, friendly people and all this space and there are Americans. Yes, I've met them. Who love it too and say they wish they could. I haven't been to New York but I've been to London and to Sydney and I don't think she should rubbish the country that gave her. I have to say it. And I admit she takes it quite well.

'Really Bea?' She looks puzzled. 'I didn't know I was doing that.'

'You do it,' I tell her. 'It happens every visit.'

'I do have some attachment to this country,' she says. 'I wasn't yelling for Uncle Sam when the America's Cup was on.'

'Maybe. But over here you're always going on about. We haven't got this. We haven't got that. We're so backward. Diddy, I like what New Zealand is.'

'You big soft thing!' she says. 'I just get homesick. I'm sorry, Bea, but I don't think of this country as home.'

'I know that.' I glance at her quick, electric grin and suspect that she's cheerful because in twenty-four hours. I look in the rear-vision mirror and then pull over into the turn-off lane. 'You are really sure about me coming over for a month?'

'Really, really sure. And please, please, do not ask me that again.'

'I have to know, Diddy, because I thought I'd see the travel agent tomorrow.'

She looks surprised but says, 'Great!'

'It's eleven months but we need time to shop around for discounted fares. So. I need to know you're positive.'

'Bea!'

'All right, all right. That's fine.' I realise I've got a touch of indigestion. It could be about New York but I think. Yes, I really am nervous about showing her Kiwiana. I'm afraid she'll. Well, really, it's the way she is about everything New Zealand. She was unhappy here. Funny how the little things. When you're travelling for instance. A bowl of cold soup, a long wait in the Post Office and you hate a country. I think she was lonely. Hell, we were both lonely. I think that's the ultimate fear. Not death. Loneliness. We are so scared of being on our. But then she got the Rhodes Scholarship. No, not Rhodes Scholarship. What am I thinking? That was Dad's joke. The scholarship to the Rhode Island School of Design and everything changed for her. As Sister Jean Baptiste used to say, nothing is chance, girls. But Diddy developed this. Well, she would call it attitude. Except she doesn't think she's got it. It's over here too, I suppose. Aucklanders and Wellingtonians hitting out at each other in competition. You don't make yourself taller standing on someone else. Diddy, you were lonely here, I want to tell her. You were dying of loneliness. That's all it was. It coloured your view of everything. But what's the use. She always knows better than anyone.

'What are you thinking?' she asks.

The suddenness of it makes me jump. 'Why do you ask?'

'You were making weird faces at the traffic.'

'If you must know, I'm scared.' I look at her. 'I think you mightn't like it.'

'Your restaurant? Why wouldn't I like it? Bea, my big regret about the last visit was that I didn't get to see your seafood place. What was it called?'

'La Mer.'

'I knew I associated it with Debussy. We planned it and our plans got changed and I said next time. Remember? Then you wrote you sold it.'

'La Mer was smaller. This is a much bigger building so I. But I don't do more than twenty tables. Over twenty you get into mass production. Everything's fresh. No frozen. No convenience foods. Sauces made from scratch. Bread baked on the. We got 8.5 from *Cuisine* magazine.'

'I'm hungry,' she says.

I doubt if it's true but I'm grateful to her for saying it like she meant it. She really is trying hard.

She is gracious to everyone. She likes the decor, she tells me. She says, oh God, she's forgotten all about things like washboards and butter churns. Where did we get the NZ Rail posters? And that's appropriate, a Buzzy Bee toy. Not a word of criticism. Not even a suggestion about design. We go out back. She looks in the fridges at the trays of lamb chops and half legs, the boned ducklings, chickens, baby salmon. She tells Margaret. I don't know whether I want to eat them or paint them, she says. She looks at everything, the pots on the rotating rail, the range of mixers, fish kettles, gas rings, ovens, vegetable bins. I'm relieved it's all right. I thought that with me being away. But it's spotless. Margaret's doing. Diddy talks to everyone. Tells Franz and Peter and Julie that she has culinary thrombosis. I'm a bloody clot in the kitchen she says and they laugh even though it's an old joke. Now she asks them to explain the marinades and sauces they're making. She tries so hard. Donald, the maitre d', thinks she's darling. That's the word he uses. Darling. He shows her over the wine stocks. He gives a history of wine-making in New Zealand and she listens. She says generally. Generally, she says, New Zealand whites are better than Californian. Oh whoop-de-doo! Chalk it up. Then the serving staff come in, all young, four of them students. I introduce her. My sister from New York. Hi. Good evening. Gee, I didn't know you were American. I'm a New Yorker, she says. New York isn't America. New York is the world. And Donald takes us to the prime table, unobstructed view of the city. No hurry, she says. We've got all evening. Then I have to say no we haven't because Kiwiana is booked out and we eat now or we eat in the kitchen. She is impressed. Booked out? Most nights, I tell her. She likes the menu. She really does like the menu. She orders Pacific oysters with a horseradish dip and a baby salmon with a raisin and almond sauce. I keep forgetting that she doesn't eat red meat.

She sips the wine and looks out the window. 'Tell me about Rawson.'

'Rawson? My chef at La Mer? Why?'

'Well, anyone,' she says. 'Any of your men friends. I realise I know so little. We are goddam awful at letter writing, aren't we? I guess it's not the sort of thing you put in letters.'

'I'll tell you about Rawson.' I start to laugh. 'The year before I sold La Mer. They asked me to be judge. The Chef of the Year Award. And we went to this big hotel in Auckland.'

'You and Rawson.'

'No, me and the other judges. Oh, Rawson was there too. The five judges were on one floor. The chefs were all on another. And in my room there was this huge king-sized.'

'Bea, no!'

'It was all right. I told him to be very careful. He understood he could be disqualified. I ordered some champagne and canapes from room service. It came on a lovely silver trolley with a little lace cloth and two glasses, red roses. I left the latch over to keep the door ajar and then.' I look out the window, remembering how he came in, so quickly and quietly, eyes laughing, how he filled his mouth with champagne and kissed it into mine.

'Go on,' says Diddy.

But I can't go on because Margaret has brought out two covered dishes. She takes the lids off some lean lamb chops and a pink salmon with scales still shining.

I explain to Diddy that we always show the customer the food before it is cooked.

'Does it ever put them off?' she asks.

'No. Never. We don't get basic with blood and feathers. People like seeing the quality and freshness. It's a feature of Kiwiana.'

Margaret replaces the lids and takes the dishes out back. Diddy leans forward and I go on, 'I think I told you. Rawson was beautiful. He had these really high round buttocks that kind of jutted out. And he was so sensitive, just so, so lovely. It was a wonderful evening. But later I got worried. He was asleep and I thought. Maybe room service would come back for the trolley. So I got up, opened the door just a bit. There was no one out there. And I pushed the trolley into the hall. The wheel stuck. I was jiggling it. Then the door.'

'Good grief, Bea!'

'Yes. It closed behind me.'

'What were you wearing?'

'Nothing, Diddy. Not a stitch. I didn't know what I

could. I tried hammering on the door. Rawson slept like a log. Then I thought supposing someone in the next room came out. What if? And my room was almost opposite the lifts. Elevators, you call them. I couldn't stand there. There was only one place. The stairs. Do you like that wine?'

'It's delicious, Bea, a great aftertaste. The stairs, you said.'

'You know, even in the poshest hotel. Stairs are terrible. Bare concrete. No heat. It was winter and I was shivering. Clothes. Where could I get clothes? I prayed about it. I really prayed. Don't laugh, Diddy, this is serious. I thought of baby Jesus wrapped in swaddling clothes and I went down two floors, shivering. The cleaners had left one of their carts. It was by the stairs door. You know the canvas bags on those carts?'

'Dirty linen?' says Diddy.

'Dirty anything is better than nothing. I got two sheets. It's surprising what you can. One sheet around the waist. Another folded over. It was like a fancy dress costume. I looked quite. Except for my bare feet. Then I went down to the lobby. Well, I had to. I needed to phone my room. You know what? The phone woke Rawson up but he was too scared to answer it. He said he saw I wasn't there. But he couldn't. He didn't. He got dressed and ran. He didn't work it out.'

'What did you do?'

'Nothing is chance, you know, Diddy. Earlier on I'd been talking to a very nice doorman. He was still on duty. He got me another key.'

'What about Rawson?' she asks.

'He won it,' she says. 'He got chef of the year and a big Auckland restaurant offered. But that's the way it is. The story of my life. Do you like that wine?'

'Yes, I told you. It's wonderful.'

'Good. It's private bin and really special.'

'Will you let me pay for it?' she asks.

'No! Goodness no! Diddy, you shouldn't even.'

'I was just trying to be practical.' She raises her glass. 'As Dad used to say, it isn't doing much for the economy.'

'That wasn't Dad. It was Uncle Jack.'

'Oh?'

'When they were shearing. Lunch breaks. Remember?'

'You're right,' she says. 'It was Uncle Jack. Bea, there used to be photos of him. Did they –'

I shake my head and she doesn't take it further.

She gazes out of the window, her face soft with thinking and then she says, 'Bea, you know I told you I had never been in love? That's not strictly the truth.'

'I know.' I nod the rest for her. 'I was in love with him too. We all were.'

We sit there, looking at the sweep of Wellington city, the buildings that tumble like children's play blocks, right down to the sea, the little boats tucked in against the wharves. In the blue sky above the eastern hills, I see a small yellow plane. I know she sees it too. It's in her New York sky as well. That same yellow plane is everywhere.

12
1953

Beatrice thought that the two worst things were getting drowned and getting undrowned but in between it was lovely, a big white light that came around her so soft and nice that she wanted to stay in it always. The next year at school, she told Sister Marcella about it and Sister Marcella said the light was an angel coming to take her to Jesus, but when the angel saw that her Mummy and Daddy were so sad, it took her back again.

Maybe getting undrowned affected Beatrice's memory because she never knew what happened the next morning. It was Sunday. They must have gone to Mass in Foxton. They never missed Mass. But she had no recollection of it at all. All she could remember was sitting on the steps of the caravan, feeling pleased that her mother had played her tune at the party the night before. She was hoping that people would look at her and say to each other that she was the child who was nearly drowned yesterday and that was her special music her mother played last night.

She remembered lunch at the picnic table and Diddy wanting a bonfire on the beach. Dad said, all right, as long as the wind didn't get up, and everyone sat eating pancakes, looking sleepy and happy, no one in a hurry to do anything. The day was warm and the pine trees smelled lovely. When the men's cigarette smoke went up into the shadows, it turned blue and twisty like the genie from Aladdin's lamp and Beatrice thought if she watched long enough, she'd see a face in it. She did see a little green beetle fly into Uncle Jack's tea. It swam around quickly and then died of hotness. When Beatrice looked next it was gone. Uncle Jack said he drank it. He said it gave the tea a special flavour like a lime green jellybean. Mum laughed and said, 'Jack you are so silly,' and Beatrice laughed too. She was happy because everyone was happy.

In the afternoon they all walked down to the skating rink. The grown-ups didn't have any skates but they watched how Diddy could go backwards and turn around without falling over. She could even lean forward and put one leg up behind her like a figure skater. Celia Upton was at the rink. But she didn't talk to Diddy and Diddy didn't talk to her. All the time they didn't look at each other. That was because of you know what.

Mum helped Beatrice to put on her skates. They were ordinary skates with black wheels and silver bits that tightened over her shoes with a key. Mum held her while she stood up and guided her to the bar. Beatrice had to put both arms on the bar because the wheels kept skidding her feet away. But it was all right. She got used to it.

Dad and Uncle Jack came over from watching Diddy skate backwards. They got on each side of Beatrice and took her onto the rink. She didn't fall because they held her up. 'Walk,' said Uncle Jack. 'Lift your feet and walk, Buzzy Bea,' and she did that, clump, clump, clump. After a while, with each clump the wheels went around. She was skating, really skating. Uncle Jack and Dad still held onto her hands, walking beside her while she went clump, slide, clump, slide. She couldn't stop laughing. 'Look at me!' Diddy in front of her, skating backwards, yelled, 'Mum! Look at Bea.' Then Mum came down with Dad's camera and she made them all stand still while she got a picture. It was just lovely.

After that, she could skate holding onto Diddy's hand. She fell over only three times and once Diddy fell too. They both laughed because their legs got criss-crossed and the grown-ups were cheering from their seats at the side.

'They look like the three bears,' said Diddy. 'Father Bear and Mother Bear and Baby Bear.'

'Which one's Baby Bear?' said Beatrice.

Diddy helped her to stand up. 'Dad's Baby Bear. Uncle Jack is taller.'

'But Dad's wider than Uncle Jack.'

'Okay,' said Diddy. 'They can be the Three Billy Goats Gruff.'

Bea laughed so hard that she fell down again.

She didn't know how long they stayed at the rink. The next thing it was late afternoon and they were putting the beach picnic stuff in the car, Mum's fold-up chair, rugs, jerseys in case it got cold, Uncle Jack's leather flying jacket.

'I'm wearing this, I'm wearing this,' said Diddy wrapping it around her until Mum made her put it back. Paper for the fire, cold drink and bottles of beer, boiled potatoes in a pot, sweetcorn, salad, tomato sauce, sausages already cooked. Mum had a loaf of bread in the caravan oven. They were waiting for it.

'Tell you what,' said Uncle Jack. 'The girls and I will cut across through the sandhills. We'll start the fire. You two drive around when the bread's done.'

'Yes! Yes! Yes!' Beatrice and Diddy jumped up and down.

'No,' said Dad. 'We'll all go together.'

'It could be half an hour,' Mum said. 'It's a slow oven.'

Dad nodded. 'All right. I'll go with the girls. You and Jack bring the car when you're ready.'

The sun was a spinning fireball close to the sea and all the air was golden. When Dad looked out to sea his face was gold-washed. So was Diddy's. There was gold on everything except for the shadows which were dark blue. Beatrice held a stick up in the air and called, 'I'm the golden sea fairy with the golden wand.'

'Don't you go near the sea,' Dad said. 'You hear me?'

He didn't need to tell her. Nothing would make her go near that hungry horrible sea that had rolled her over and over so she couldn't breathe.

There was a lot of dry wood on the beach. They stacked little bits over some paper and Dad set fire to it with his cigarette lighter. In the gold light, the flame was almost colourless. Diddy and Beatrice handed Dad more wood and he added them, one bit at a time, to the pile. When at last the car came roaring up the beach, toot, toot, toot, the fire was huge with orange and green sparks floating up into the darkening sky.

Mum had the bread wrapped in a tea towel. They could smell it as soon as she got out of the car. She kissed Dad and then broke off a piece of the warm crust and put it in his mouth. He loved fresh bread. He told her to give Jack some too. So she broke another bit off for Uncle Jack.

Uncle Jack screwed up his face and pretended to cry. 'Where's my kiss? I didn't get my kiss.'

'Don't talk like that,' said Mum.

'My kiss!' wailed Uncle Jack.

'Frank? Tell him not to be so stupid,' said Mum. But she was laughing and so was Dad.

The men put out Mum's chair and told her to sit down. They put a rug over her knees and said she could be the queen and they would be her slaves. They were in a real jokey mood, teasing her and each other. They unpacked the car and set out the food on a cloth. They put the pots of sausages and corn beside the fire. There was nothing for Beatrice and Diddy to do, so they went down the beach and looked for shells until it was too dark to see. Above the horizon, the sky was dark red. Diddy said the day was bleeding to death because the sun had gone. But from a distance, it looked as though a bit of the sun had fallen onto the beach, the bonfire was so big and bright. Beatrice made up a story about the bonfire being a lighthouse saving a ship at sea.

Then they heard the music. Uncle Jack had brought his little wind-up gramophone. He had it in the boot of the car and was playing a 78 rpm record. It was Gene Autrey or Slim Whitman, one of those, a cowboy song with lots of yodelling. Beatrice thought it was strange for a dark beach to get filled up with music. The fish would listen. The seagulls and crabs. Maybe even the stars would hear it.

'You have my heart, dear, and this you know. So tell me why you treat it so. I gave it to you. T'was my mistake. Remember darling, that hearts do break. Oh-de, oh-de, lay-ee-dee.'

Mum was in her chair. Dad and Uncle Jack were sitting together on the log, drinking beer and swaying to the music. The firelight on their faces made them look lovely, like the picture of Jesus in The Light of the World.

'Here come my princesses,' said Uncle Jack. 'Princess Delia and Princess Beatrice. Come and sit down.'

Diddy and Bea ran for the space beside Uncle Jack but Diddy got there first and plonked herself down. She gave Beatrice a ha-ha look. That was all right. Beatrice got between

Dad and Uncle Jack and wriggled and wriggled until Dad moved over to let her sit. She leaned forward to smile at Diddy. She had both of them, so there.

'Look!' said Mum. 'The moon!'

'About a quarter full,' said Dad. 'That should mean good fishing tomorrow.'

'It's a rocking horse,' said Diddy. 'You can't see the horse though. It's as black as the sky.'

'I think it's a smiley mouth,' said Beatrice.

'Well,' said Uncle Jack. 'It's looks like a bit of toenail to me.' He got up to change the record and Beatrice and Diddy were left with empty space between them.

'Toenail!' laughed Mum. 'How romantic!'

'What do you expect from an old bush pilot?' said Uncle Jack, winding the handle on his gramophone. 'You hear that, Frank? Her majesty thinks I'm unromantic.'

'Jack!' Mum put her hand over her mouth. She turned to Dad. 'Frank, this terrible man twists every word I say.'

'What will we do with him, eh Agnes?' Dad reached out and grabbed Mum's hand.

'I think we should make him get in his plane and fly back to Australia,' said Mum.

'Good idea,' said Dad.

Beatrice leaned forward, her chin on her hand. She hated it when grown-ups made pretend talk. She was pleased when Uncle Jack said, 'Fat bloody chance!' and put the needle down on the record.

'At the beach at Waikiki, just my little honey bunny and me . . .'

Dad brought out the forks made from twisted number eight wire and they put sausages on the end. The fire had burned down to an orange lumpiness which was very hot. Uncle Jack said it was a good thing that the forks were long or the sausages they'd be eating would be called princess fingers. He and Dad served up the potatoes and corn and salad and handed around the serviettes.

'– telling my love with a ukulele tune, under a honey bunny Honolulu moon.'

The girls dropped two sausages into the fire and Mum said wonderful, only two? Everyone dropped sausages. The important thing was did they have enough left over and yes, they had, so who cared?

'Everything's hunky-dory,' said Uncle Jack.

Beatrice and Diddy dipped sausages and potatoes into the tomato sauce and drank lemonade straight from the bottles and then Diddy wanted to tell ghost stories. Dad said, 'Why not just listen to the music?' Diddy said they always told ghost stories when they had a bonfire, that was part of it. The grown-ups took no notice. Uncle Jack put on one record after another and Diddy didn't like to argue too much with Uncle Jack.

When the fire got right down, Dad threw on a couple of bits of wood and they played some dance music. Uncle Jack bowed low in front of Mum's chair and asked her if she would like to do a turn around the dance floor. She shook her head. 'Go on,' said Dad, but she still said no. So Uncle Jack bowed in front of Dad and Dad got up. They had an argument about who was going to lead. They couldn't get started. They had arms on each other and arms stuck up in the air. Diddy said they looked like a teapot. The music finished and Uncle Jack wound it up again.

'You're bloody useless,' he said to Dad and they laughed and laughed.

'Dance with me!' cried Diddy, jumping up and running to Uncle Jack.

They danced, the four of them, Diddy with Uncle Jack,

Beatrice with Dad, on the cold dark sand at the edge of the firelight. It was thumpy music that made Beatrice's feet stamp up and down, sometimes on Dad's toes, and her head wag from side to side. When the music got faster, Dad picked her up and hugged her and twirled her so her face was on his shoulder. She looked to see if Diddy was being twirled by Uncle Jack. She wasn't. Diddy was doing real dancing, with Uncle Jack telling her what to do with her feet. Then the music and dancing stopped and Mum clapped, crying out, 'Bravo! Bravo!'

Dad said it was time to go. The tide was coming up. Mum folded her chair and blanket. The plates were scraped onto the fire and stacked inside the pot. Bottles were picked up. Serviettes and sauce. All of it went back in the boot of the car with the gramophone which once more looked like a small suitcase.

Uncle Jack got in the car and started it. It moved forward, then back and the wheels spun. He got out and looked. 'I need your help, Frank. We're in a bit of loose sand.'

Dad bent over to look at the back of the car. 'A push should do it. Agnes, you get in. Put it in second and use the clutch. We'll rock it out.'

Dad, Uncle Jack, Diddy and Beatrice, put their weight against the back of the car. The engine made a loud noise as though it was hurting and the wheels spun, throwing sand back at them. Then the car sank down, even lower than before.

'Stop!' yelled Dad.

'Too much bloody throttle,' muttered Uncle Jack. 'We're really stuck.'

'What do you want me to do now?' Mum called.

'Nothing, dear,' said Dad. 'Just come out. We're right down on the axle. We'll have to think of something else.'

Mum stood with Diddy and Beatrice while Dad and Uncle Jack went around the car, bending down, looking, talking about the tide.

Uncle Jack said, 'I'll whizz back to the camp. There'll be someone there to pull us out.'

'Not with this tide,' said Dad. 'They wouldn't risk it. It'll have to be a tractor.'

Uncle Jack began to roll a cigarette. 'Where the blazes do you get a tractor this time of night?'

'There's that bloke,' said Dad. 'He launches boats.'

'Not at night,' said Uncle Jack.

'He's got a farm down Beach Road. He'll come. He does this sort of thing. Skipper, his name is. Skipper Emanuel. It's a bit of a walk.'

'I'll go,' said Uncle Jack. 'Tell me where it is.'

They argued for a bit. Dad said he'd go because he knew the farm. Uncle Jack said, no, he should go because he'd got them in this shit, pardon his French. Dad said it would be better for Jack to stay with the car. Agnes and the girls could go back to the caravan. No, said Mum, she didn't fancy the idea of going through the sandhills in the dark. They would all stay at the car. Then Uncle Jack asked, was Dad sure they couldn't get a tow from the camping ground and Dad said with what? Look at the tide.

'Well, I'll get the bloke with the tractor,' said Uncle Jack, 'and that's final. A man should stay with his family.'

'You don't know where it is,' said Dad.

'Then bloody tell me,' said Uncle Jack, and Dad said, 'Where's the torch, I'm going.'

Dad walked away, the light at his back quickly fading so that after a while all they saw was the occasional sweep of the torch. They sat on the log, Diddy, Uncle Jack, Mum, Beatrice, and it was so quiet they could hear the breathing of the sea and the small noises of the collapsing embers. The fire was dying and the darkness was huge.

Mum looked first at Beatrice, then at Diddy. 'What dirty faces! And your hands! Have you two seen yourselves?'

Beatrice studied her hands. She wiped her mouth with her knuckles.

Mum went to the car, opened and closed a door and came back with a towel. 'Now. Go down to the edge of the sea, both of you. Dip the corner of the towel in the water. Wash your faces and hands, then dry yourselves with the rest of it.'

'I'll do it back at the camp,' said Diddy.

'You'll do it now,' said Mum. 'You're filthy. I'm not having you in the car like that.'

'We haven't got the torch,' said Beatrice. She looked to Uncle Jack for support but he was just smoking and looking at the fire.

'The tide's half in,' said Mum. 'It's not very far.'

'But it's dark!' she cried.

'Go on,' said Mum. 'Diddy'll be with you.'

Diddy snatched the towel from Mum and walked ahead towards the sea. Beatrice ran to catch up before the dark grabbed her. She reached for Diddy's arm but Diddy shook her off, so Beatrice hung onto the end of the towel. The sky, sand and water were all as black as black and she couldn't even see where she was putting her feet. Diddy was scared too, because she was walking slower. The only way they knew there was water in front of them was the breathing noise which was getting louder, waves going in and out, in and out. Beatrice was filled with the fear of yesterday, the sensation of falling and the sea rolling her back along the rough sand. When she added that to the darkness, she knew she could not go any further. She stopped and began to cry. 'Dad told me not to go near the sea!'

'Dad did say that!' said Diddy. 'He did. I heard him.' She grabbed Beatrice's hand. They turned and ran back towards the small glow of the fire, the towel trailing in the sand behind them.

Mum and Uncle Jack were not on the log. They were not anywhere. Diddy walked to the car, pulling Bea along with one hand, the towel with the other. That's where they found them. Mum and Uncle Jack. They were leaning against the other side of the car and they were kissing. Mum's hands were on the back of Uncle Jack's head and neck and his arms were around her. It was a long kiss.

Maybe there was a noise. Perhaps Mum saw the girls. Suddenly, she pushed Uncle Jack away and turned, one hand holding the car door. 'You didn't wash!' she said to Diddy.

Beatrice thought that Diddy would explain but Diddy didn't say anything. She just stood there, the towel hanging in the sand.

Uncle Jack rubbed his eye. 'Well, I reckon that's taken care of it. Can't feel anything.' He looked at Diddy and Beatrice. 'I got a bit of sand in my eye. Your mother was just getting it out for me.'

Mum said, 'These two are always getting things in their eyes. They know what it's like.'

'Sure feels better,' said Uncle Jack, blinking one eye, then the other in a way that twisted his mouth.

Still Diddy did not speak.

Beatrice said, 'I was scared. Dad said don't go near the water.'

'Oh,' said Mum. 'Of course!' She took the towel from Diddy, shook it and folded it. 'I'm sorry, Bea. I was forgetting. You can wash back at the camping ground.'

'When is Dad coming?' Beatrice wanted to know.

'He'll be a little while yet,' said Mum. 'He has to go to

Mr Emanuel's farm. Why don't we sit on the log and have a singsong?' She held their arms and guided them back to the fire and they sat down on either side of her. 'Who wants to start?' she said.

'I know an old lady who swallowed a fly,' said Beatrice.

Uncle Jack stood behind them. He put his fingertips down hardly touching Mum's shoulders. He said, 'Sure as eggs, there's someone at the camp can give us a tow. I'm going to ask.' Then he turned and walked towards the sandhills.

Beatrice started, 'I know an old lady who swallowed a fly. I don't know why she swallowed a fly.'

Mum stood up. 'I'd better go too. You know what Uncle Jack's like. He'll probably get lost. Listen. I want you two to sit in the car. All right? Stay in the car and don't get out. Your Dad's right. No one at the camp will come to our rescue. But that's Uncle Jack for you. We'll be back before you know it.' She opened the door, guided them into the back seat and gave them her blanket. Diddy promptly pushed it onto the floor.

'If Dad does come back first, just tell him what Uncle Jack said. We're looking for help.' She smiled. 'Don't get out of the car, whatever you do. I won't be long.'

Beatrice sat forward to watch her walk quickly, awkwardly through the sand in her wedge-heeled sandals. Further over, almost hidden in the darkness, stood Uncle Jack.

It was cold in the car and Diddy had thrown the rug on the floor. Beatrice leaned over to the front seat and got Uncle Jack's flying jacket. She pulled it over and draped it across her shoulders, chest and stomach. 'I'm having this,' she said.

For once, Diddy didn't argue. She just sat there, hitting the back of her left hand with a bit of shell or stick. Beatrice couldn't quite see what. It must have really hurt, but Beatrice didn't say anything because that would only make Diddy do it all the more. So she said, 'Do you want to sing?'

Diddy didn't want to sing. Hit, hit, hit.

Beatrice sang all the verses of 'I Know an Old Lady' and she was starting on 'Coming Round the Mountain' when Dad arrived. They didn't see him come back. He gave them a fright with the sudden sweep of his torchlight over the car.

He tapped on Diddy's window and she wound it down. 'We're in luck,' he said. 'The tractor was on the beach and Mr Emanuel was in the store. He'll be down soon.' He pulled his head out of the window and looked to left and right. 'Where are they?'

'Camping ground,' said Bea. 'They went to get a car to tow us.'

Dad waved his arms about. 'What did they do that for? I told Jack. It's a tractor or nothing. They shouldn't have left.' His hands opened and closed. 'Well, I'd better get back. Mr Emanuel will be waiting for me to show him the way.' He took a couple of steps backwards. 'Are you two all right?'

Diddy had not said a word but now she opened the car door and got out. She walked to the front of the car and stood, her hands on her hips, facing Dad. He stopped. Beatrice could see them both, dark shapes with just a ribbon of pale firelight on them. She heard Diddy say, 'They were kissing. Dad! They were kissing!' Then Diddy turned and got back into the car.

Dad took another two steps backwards and stopped. He put his head down and kicked the sand, one foot, then the other, kick, kick. He walked over to the fire for no reason, kicked more sand, and walked back again. He leaned on the front of the car as though he was going to push it backwards and then he turned and marched towards the sandhills.

Beatrice slid down under the leather flying jacket and rocked from side to side. 'He got sand in his eye. He got sand in his eye. He got sand in his eye.'

'Shut up!' said Diddy.

It was a long time. Or was it a little time? Beatrice didn't know. The fire was almost out, just a bit of orange here and there winking like goblin eyes, and someone was running in the darkness, out of breath. Beatrice thought it was Dad opening the driver's door. But she saw the outline of hair and it was curly. And it was a different smell. Strong. Like the farm dogs. He was breathing really hard. His hand was going over the front seat and floor, touching things. Then he reached up and switched on the inside light. Beatrice made a quick hup noise. She couldn't help it. Uncle Jack was hurt. He had black stuff coming out of his nose and more black on his lip and chin. One eyelid was right down over his eye and he looked awful. Just awful, awful, awful.

'Sorry, Buzzy Bea.' He didn't even sound like Uncle Jack. He took the flying jacket off her, put out the light and closed the door. Everything was dark. She didn't see where he went.

'Diddy?' she said. 'Diddy?'

Her sister was not moving. She was singing very softly, 'I know an old lady who swallowed a fly.'

There were other things about that day that Beatrice could not remember. Later, she put it down to the near-drowning and thought that oxygen starvation probably caused some kind of short circuit. She didn't remember her parents getting into the car. She didn't remember the tractor arriving. It must have come and obviously they were towed off the beach without any damage to the old Chevrolet. It must have taken them a while to get back to the camping ground and pack. All of that was missing. The only other thing she remembered was the road to Napier and the way it flowed like a river towards the lights of the car. They were driving slowly, the caravan bumping along behind them and no one was talking. Mum sat straight and still in the front passenger seat. They couldn't even see her breathing. It was Dad who was crying. His big hands held onto each side of the wheel and every now and then a terrible noise came out of him. It was different from the way Mum or Diddy or Beatrice cried. It was bigger. Like someone dying. It shook him through and through.

Diddy lay in the backseat corner, the rug pulled over her head. Maybe she was asleep. Beatrice sat with her thumb in her mouth, watching the river of road. It seemed as though the holiday was over. No one had said so. No one had explained anything and it was all too big for questions.

13
DELIA

It's the first time Bea and I have talked about it. Really talked.

We are sitting on the beach not far from Bea's back fence and it's dark enough for the lights of Wellington to twinkle like fireflies across the water. The sea and hills, sliding into evening, have an edge to them that suggests they are one step removed from reality. It would take an artist like Jackson Pollock or maybe the composer Erik Satie to trickle the melting colours and shapes into an abstract composition.

'Why did you do it?' Bea asks.

We have a wine bottle anchored in the sand and a couple of glasses carried from the house, sheer excess because we have already had wine with an excellent dinner.

'Why did I do it? I'm not sure, Bea. It could be that I don't want to know, but I think I genuinely don't know. Children are not reflective. They don't analyse and name their emotions. My feelings as a child were like strong winds. They seemed to come from nowhere and go nowhere, battering me in passing. That night I had a tornado inside me. That's all I can say for certain.'

'The thing is,' says Bea, 'we all loved him so much. Both Mum and Dad. She must have all the time she was ignoring.

And you and I. He was such. I think he was the most lovable man I have ever met.'

'I could call it jealousy.' I tell her. 'But that's too simple. Emotions are rarely as distinct as our rational evaluation makes them. Do you realise that it was almost exactly forty-five years ago?'

She sips her wine in silence and I suspect that we are both wondering how an event that old could happen only last night in our memory. If we lived for another forty-five years, I guess it would still be as recent.

'The silence was the worst thing,' says Bea. 'Like a great black hole in the house. You felt you always had to watch. It was always there. You were scared it would swallow you up.'

I too, remember the silence and how careful they were with each other. 'I suppose you realise that if it happened now, it wouldn't even be worthy of gossip?'

'I asked them once,' she says. 'When you were in Auckland. It was one of those awful silent dinners and I asked. "What became of Uncle Jack?" I said. No one said anything. I asked again. "Dad, what happened to Uncle Jack?" He said, "We don't talk about that." "Why?" I said. "We just don't," he said. She didn't say a word. But I remember. I remember this. They both looked terrible. Not angry. More like I'd just given them a death sentence. Diddy, are you hot? Or is it just my flushes?'

'It's a warm night.'

'Once,' she says. 'Once when Dad was in town at the saleyards. I came off the school bus. I heard her. She was playing that music.'

'The "Moonlight"?'

'No, no.' Bea clicks her fingers. '"Black and White Rag". But she stopped when she saw me walk past the window. I never heard it again.'

'Did they ever mention him in later years?'

'Not that I know of. I really don't think they talked at all. You know, between themselves. If they did they might have. It went on for so long. They seemed stuck. Heck, it's hot. We should have a swim. Not that they ever really talked to us, either. Mum said more to Mrs Rawiri than to me. Maybe that was because Mrs Rawiri didn't understand much English.' She laughs, then says, 'You still haven't told me about your Italian dressing gown. Your robe.'

'Yes, I did.'

'No, you didn't. You started. You never finished.'

'I did! Oh. Didn't I? It's not much of a story. Not as good as your hotel sheets.'

'Tell me,' she says, refilling her sand-encrusted glass.

'There's really nothing to it. It was decades ago. I bought this very expensive robe and I made the mistake of leaving it on the bathroom door. I came home one afternoon. Lal was out. Sitting at the table was this young guy I'd never seen before. He was drinking coffee and wearing my robe.'

'Oh-oh!' says Bea.

'Too damned right! I was furious. I practically snatched it off him. He grabbed a dishtowel to cover himself. A dishtowel! Well, this is the lunatic bit. I went out into the street and stuffed the robe into the nearest trash bin. My gorgeous robe. Pure silk brocade.'

'Why?'

'I don't know why. When Lal came home, we went out and looked for it. It was gone, of course.' I hug my knees and stare through my glass at the city lights which blur and wink in the semillon blanc.

'What happened then?'

'Nothing. It was gone, bye-bye, no more. I told you it was a nothing story. Do you want a swim?'

'It'd be lovely,' she says, not moving.

I put down my glass, stand up, kick off my shoes, and walk towards the water in my stockinged feet.

'I've got a spare.' She is struggling up. 'Diddy, what are you?'

'Come on. Race you in.'

She hesitates. I think she is laughing or protesting. Or both. She teeters as she steps out of her shoes. The next thing, she's thumping across the sand, arms pumping like train pistons, and we're both splashing into the sea. We dive together and come up, our clothes floating around us. The water is surprisingly warm and it occurs to me that this is the first time we've been in the sea together since her near-drowning incident.

She says, 'I suppose that suit cost as much as the Italian robe.'

'Not quite.'

'You're mad, Diddy. You're absolutely mad.'

'What a nice compliment. Thank you.' I float on my back and look at the stars which are faint yet, in a violet sky rimmed with black hills. At my feet are the lights of the bay. The water bears me easily in a gentle rocking motion, up and down, up and down, and then something happens. A vast and silent music. For an instant I have the knowledge of being held, one small note in a perfect symphony. Yes, perfection. There is undeniable truth in the experience, like the presence of Dad in my office. I am the small note but I am also the entire symphony, as is Bea and the water, the hills, the sky, Lal, Dad, Mum. As is Uncle Jack. And nowhere, nowhere at all, is there a note out of place. This is the sensation that fills me with perfect knowledge, but the moment I try to analyse it, it disappears and I am once more an aging woman in an Anne Klein tussore silk suit, floating on her back in the dark of Wellington Harbour.

Bea says, 'It's definitely okay for Christmas?'

'Definitely.'

'Good. I'll come for a month. Isn't this water delicious? I'm Ophelia and you're the Lady of Shalott. We'll float the rest of our lives away.'

'The Lady of Shalott was in a boat,' I tell her.

'No, she wasn't. She was in a river.'

'She was in a boat and the boat was in the river.'

'The mirror cracked from side to side,' Bea says. 'I learned it at school.'

'The boat was drifting down the river.'

'There was no boat,' she says. 'Diddy! No boat.'

'Bea, there was.'

'There wasn't.'

We are quiet for a while. The small waves lift us, stirring our hands and our wet clothing.

Bea tips her head back a little. 'I used to think the stars were holes. When I was young. There were little holes in the sky and heaven was shining through. It didn't make me happy. It made me scared. Heaven was so far away. I didn't know how I could climb up that high. I thought maybe. Maybe there was an aeroplane that took us there.'

We both stare at the sky and I find the Southern Cross hanging over the horizon like a lopsided kite. It's years since I've seen the Southern Cross.

Bea says, 'Those old teachings about heaven and hell were just awful, weren't they?'

'Yes, they were. I think the truth is probably very simple. We are all a part of the ultimate reality. When we know that, we live in heaven. When we don't know it, we can suffer hell. The trouble is, we mess up everything with words.'

'We do, don't we? Oh heck, I'm getting water in my ears.' She stands up and raises her arms to wring out her hair. The

213

sea pours from her sleeves. 'Yes, you're right. That's about it.'

'Music's easier.' I stand too, and pull down my suit blouse which is around my armpits. 'Do you remember the pride in his voice when he used to tell people that his wife only played classical music? He wouldn't have known the classical period from romantic or baroque. It was just something he said.'

'It describes them, you know,' says Bea. 'Classical music. It was what they were.'

'Mum and Dad? I don't understand.'

'Don't ask me to explain,' she says. 'I've had too much to drink to explain anything.'

We walk out of the water together, our clothes sagging. The sand is cool now and the air has a crispness that makes our skin tingle. 'Aaron was telling me this story. A very famous old rabbi lay dying, and there was a long line of young rabbis waiting by his bed to hear his last words. You know, the last words of a man like that are ultimate wisdom. The old man's lips moved. The young rabbi by the bed bent over. "Life is like a river," said the old man.'

'Life is like a river.' Bea tosses her wet hair. 'We're very philosophical tonight.'

'It's the wine. Do you want me to finish the story?'

'I thought you had.'

'No. There's more. It went down the line, one rabbi to the next. "He says life is like a river." It got to the last rabbi in the line and he said, "What does he mean, life is like a river." Well, back that went. What does he mean? What does he mean? And the young rabbi leaning over the old man, said, "What do you mean, life is like a river?" The old man feebly waved his hand. "Life is not like a river." he said.'

'Is that the end?'

'Yes.'

She starts to laugh. She walks up the beach, slapping her thighs. 'It's not funny. It's not anything. I don't know why I am.'

I squelch after her. My clothes drip and the feet of my pantyhose become encrusted with sand. 'I like it,' I say. 'If you have to use words, they're as good as any.'

She stops and puts her hands on her hips. 'Life is like a river. Life is not like a river. Oh Diddy, both and exactly. Isn't it? All so funny and lovely and marvellous and so bloody awful at the same time.'

'Yes, Bea.' I try to find my shoes in the dark. 'That's the way it is.'